Other Books By
David Michael Slater

Picture Books
CHEESE LOUISE!
THE RING BEAR
JACQUES & SPOCK
NED LOSES HIS HEAD
MISSY SWISS!
THE SHARPEST TOOL IN THE SHED
COMIN' THROUGH
7 ATE 9
FLOUR GIRL
THE BORED BOOK

Adult Fiction
SELFLESS
THE BOOK OF LETTERS (COLLECTION)

The
Book of
Nonsense

David Michael Slater

Children's Brains are Yummy Books
Austin, Texas

Children's Brains are Yummy Books
www.childrensbrainsareyummy.com

The Book of Nonsense
Sacred Books, Volume I

Copyright © 2008 David Michael Slater

ISBN (10): 1-933767-00-6
ISBN (13): 978-1-933767-00-0

Rights Department
CBAY Books
PO Box 92411
Austin, TX 78709

Library of Congress CIP data available.

For Heidi,
who puts up with volumes of nonsense.

Contents

For every rational line or forthright statement there are leagues of senseless cacophony, verbal nonsense, and incoherency.... The impious maintain that nonsense is normal in the Library and that the reasonable...is an almost miraculous exception.

— Jorge Luis Borges —

the abc's of the abc

It was downright embarrassing to get treated so shabbily, especially after the way she'd gone on about how great the place was. Daphna's father hadn't even gotten out of his taxi before she'd announced the big news: a rare bookshop had opened in the Village while he'd been away.

"It took over that entire warehouse, the one that's been boarded up forever!" Daphna had enthused. She'd forgotten to bother with 'Welcome home,' or even 'Hello.' "It's called The Antiquarian Book Center, but I call it the ABC. It's incredible! It's huge! It's the most amazing shop I've ever seen! And what's really weird is that every single book in there has to do with magic, not that I'm really into that sort of thing, but still! In all your years as a book scout, I'll bet you've never seen anything like it, Dad. There's definitely nothing like it in Portland."

Daphna knew Milton would want to investigate, though maybe not twenty seconds after getting home from such a long trip. Six weeks was by far his longest scouting mission ever. But he admitted to having a number of books to sell around town, as well as a rather unusual item he was anxious to learn more about. When Daphna heard this, she'd insisted they take it straight to the ABC. So here they were, standing among the musty, cramped shelves in the entry of the glorious place.

The problem was they'd been standing there for several minutes, waiting to get the attention of the frighteningly large, pale boy at the front desk. Daphna saw the boy almost every time she went in, and she'd been in every day since the shop opened four weeks earlier. As usual, he was hunched over with his head down, flipping through a number of books spread out around him. There were nine on this occasion. Directly below his chin, also as usual, sat a large old leather-bound ledger with some sort of list running down its pages. Daphna had only seen the boy add something to it once or twice, even though he always clutched a pen while he read.

Milton cleared his throat for the eighth time, but the boy just kept ignoring him. He might have gone on doing so forever had Daphna not inched forward to get a closer look at what he was doing. As she leaned over the ledger, the boy slammed it shut. Then he grinned in a positively bestial way and jerked his head up. Daphna jumped back. When the boy's eyes met hers, she couldn't help herself—she screamed.

Even Milton let out a short, shocked exhalation. The boy's eyes were ravaged. They were the color of blood and seemed nearly lifeless, sagging into smudge-black bags beneath them. Daphna was glad she'd never attracted his attention before; if she had, her summer vacation might've been spent investigating old books on the Internet.

"Mind your own business, girl," the boy hissed, staring directly into Daphna's flecked green eyes. Then, grinning, he looked her over from her black bob down to her old white sneakers and whispered, "I bet it's gonna be you."

Daphna was too shaken to react, but Milton stepped forward. He cleared his throat once again and explained, rather tersely, that he was a well-respected dealer of rare books with an unusual item he might consider selling if the store's buyer was available.

"Give it," the boy demanded, jabbing out a giant hand. "I got to make sure nobody wastes the old man's time."

Daphna saw her father bristle. He probably wanted to get away from this ghastly creature almost as much as she did, but she simply had to share this place with him. "Go ahead, Dad," she urged.

Grudgingly, Milton produced from his

shoulder sack a book wrapped in a long, sheer cloth. The cloth took some time to unwind, and Milton grimaced a bit as he worked it off. Daphna felt a pang of remorse for not letting him relax after his travels. His arthritis was probably killing him from the plane and cab rides, not to mention the cool August weather he'd come home to. When the cloth was finally free, Milton set the book on the desk.

Daphna had seen her father sell some strange books over the years, but never anything like this. It was long and thin, like a thick menu—but that was only slightly unusual. She'd recently seen a book of that shape, though she couldn't remember where. What was unprecedented, for a supposedly salable book, was its brutalized condition. The book's cover was blackened, cracked, battered and gashed. The pages were warped, as if they'd once been drenched, yet their edges were charred and flaked, as if the book had, at some other time, barely escaped a fire.

Furthermore, while it appeared to be some kind of journal, the book was apparently filled with nonsense. On the short drive over to the ABC, Daphna had briefly inspected one of the brittle, handwritten pages. What she could make out appeared to be a jumble of outlandish looking foreign languages, but it was impossible to tell because everything looked blurry. Daphna never could read in the car without getting dizzy, so she'd carefully wrapped the book back up.

The boy snatched the book off the desk and began flipping through it as if it were no more valuable than a brand new comic. Daphna was sure he was going to obliterate it with his brutish hands. "Ah, get this pile of junk outta—" he started to sneer, but he was interrupted by a series of smacking sounds coming from somewhere deep in the store.

Daphna and her father both looked up over the shelves that enclosed the front room, but the noise stopped. The boy snapped the book shut and shoved it back at Milton.

"Who cares," he snorted. "Go show it to the old man. Cubby's in the center of the store, behind the curtain." But rather than lead them, or at least tell them which way to go, he slipped on a pair of dark, wrap-around sunglasses and said, "Tell 'em Emmet went hunting." He headed for the door but paused briefly in front of Daphna. "See ya tomorrow," he said in a knowing way that made her skin crawl. Then he was gone.

It was disturbing to learn that boy knew she came in every day, but then again, it wasn't that surprising. "Sorry, Dad," said Daphna, shrugging off the creeps.

Milton looked irked but peered with interest down one of the book-lined halls leading into the heart of the store. They branched out from nine places around the entry room. Daphna could tell he was getting the notion he'd underestimated the size of the place.

"Follow me!" Daphna said. And before anything else could derail them, she set off into one of the narrow halls. Her father trailed behind on his collection of rickety joints. Immediately, the pair was swallowed up by books, a universe of books. Books of all shapes and sizes were everywhere—beside them, above them, below them. There were no walls inside the warehouse. Rather, it was partitioned by massive shelving units, which angled this way and that, making it impossible to predict where any aisle led. Tangled passageways turned every which way, and they all opened into six-sided nooks and niches brimming with mysterious old volumes. When Daphna peered over the tops of any row, she could see simultaneously through dozens of "rooms" and "halls." Evidently her father had discovered the same kaleidoscopic effect because, as they wandered among the packed and looming shelves, he was uttering quiet expressions of awe.

Daphna took in a series of long, deep breaths, savoring the familiar nose-tingling scent of old books. It was a complicated smell: worn leather and threadbare cloth;

crinkled pages stained by countless fingers and the innumerable foods and drinks they smeared. It was the smell of flights of fancy and of people's very lives. It was the smell of Time, Daphna thought, and it was a smell she'd known all her life. It made her feel alive.

But of course it wasn't smells that made Daphna love books. No, it was the words themselves. It was mind-blowing to think that you could learn absolutely anything in the world if you just had the right words in the right order.

"Slow down, Daph," Milton called from somewhere.

Daphna stopped. She'd gotten used to roaming aimlessly through the ABC, trusting her reliable instincts to lead her around. But this was not a good plan with her father, who was having an especially difficult time because books were piled practically every few steps in tilting towers on the floor.

When he caught up, Daphna looked at

him closely for the first time since he'd arrived home. He seemed not so much tired as distant or distracted.

It has to be Dex, she realized. Her brother had intentionally not been home when the cab arrived, and Milton hadn't even asked about him. He was obviously too upset! Dexter knew the cab was coming some time after breakfast, yet he still chose to go out loitering, or whatever it was he did all day. Not being there was his way of punishing their father, she assumed, for scouting all summer. Daphna certainly hadn't been happy about it either, but she wasn't going to sulk. She understood that when a scout gets onto promising leads, he's got to follow them. And besides, Milton did get home before their birthday—even if he only made it by a day. Daphna could hardly wait to find out what he had planned.

As long as she could remember, he'd talked about how important the thirteenth birthday was in a person's life and how they'd do something really special when it came.

"Sorry, Dad," Daphna said, watching her father recover his breath.

They trudged on, now at an even slower pace, taking one blind turn after another among the books.

Daphna, growing excited again, began pointing out sections they passed. "Those books are all on Wizardry," she declared, waving a finger. "Oh, those are Sorcery and Enchantment. These, all these, are on Conjuration." She pronounced this last word with some gravity, having just the other day looked it up.

"Over there, Dad—those are manuals for casting charms, spells and hexes. Don't know what any of those books over there are. Never seen that section, either. Oh, up ahead is an aisle full of biographies of witches and warlocks. I think, earlier, all those annoying piles—those were handbooks for identifying amulets and talismans. Somewhere back there was a section of instruction books for wands and staffs. Crazy, isn't it?"

To Daphna, magic was a childish pur-
suit, but she had to admit the books in this
place looked enchanted all collected together,
glowing ever so slightly under the dim and
dusty light thrown off by the flickering lamps
hanging overhead.

"Spectacular," Milton puffed. "Never
seen anything like it. But I'm afraid I'm getting a bit—Well, now!" They had just taken
one more in a seemingly endless series of
haphazard turns, but now they found themselves in front of a heavy maroon curtain
hanging between two especially large shelving units. "I was beginning to think we were
going in circles," Milton sighed.

Daphna meant to admit fearing the
same, but her eyes were drawn to an opening
in the curtain. Just visible through it was the
silhouette of a stooped and frail man sitting
at a desk in the dark. She felt an unaccount-
able stab of panic at the sight.

A match was struck inside the cubby,

and two candles were lit by a pair of trembling hands.

"Come in! Come in, my good man," croaked a ragged, rasping voice. "I'd love to have a word with you."

only the rain

While his sister and father were no doubt drooling together in some lame bookstore, probably that new one Daphna had been practically living in all summer, Dexter Wax ranged over the many unpaved roads of Multnomah Village. It wasn't really a 'village,' of course. That was just a rustic name for their neighborhood, specifically for the row of antique shops—junk shops in Dex's opinion—running along the main street. Dexter had an atrocious sense of direction, but he loved to walk, and he didn't care about getting lost for a while. The way he figured it, you can't miss what you don't aim for.

No way, no how, was he going to sit around waiting for his father. Why should he, just to watch Milton get all jazzed up with

Daphna about how much a pile of useless old books might be worth? And so what if it was their first chance to spend time together in over a month. He'd probably leave right away for another trip, anyway. Dex would just say he forgot what time the cab was coming. And so what if he never forgot details like that? There was a first time for everything. If his dad actually was planning something for their supposedly big-deal thirteenth birthday, Dex thought it would be ideal if he could manage to "forget" to be there for that, too. Maybe he'd sneak out of the house before everyone got up tomorrow morning.

Scraggles of ripped material flicked from the holes in his jeans as Dex passed the Multnomah Village Post Office and merged onto the path that led into Gabriel Park. It was going to rain any minute, but that annoyance didn't even register. He was too agitated about having his last week of freedom messed up to worry about darkening skies. He needed some time in the Clearing.

Off the trail ahead was a path he'd forged in the woods last year. It was the first day Dex had ever skipped school, so he'd been looking for a place to hide. The good thing about middle school was that the teachers were far too busy to apply much pressure to a kid who barely scraped by, as long as he didn't bother anyone.

Of course Dex had gotten lost as soon as he'd gone into the woods that day, but while looking for a way out, he'd come upon a circular clearing ringed by a group of interesting trees. In the springtime some of them had greenish flowers hanging from them. It was like stepping into another world, a quiet, peaceful world, all leaves and branches and birds.

Dex had been going there several times a week all vacation long to watch seedpods spinning in the breeze when they fell. There was nowhere else he could go to get away from all the nags in his life. He could go see Ruby, of course, his secret friend at the rest home. She understood him, but going there was always dicey since Daphna might be around at any time doing her stupid good deeds.

Absorbed by a rising tide of hostility, Dex hurried on with his head down, watching the path pass beneath his shoes.

There was a second in which Dex saw the other shoe. It was huge, but there was no time to react. He collided with its owner, someone massive, and went crashing to the ground.

The next thing he knew, Dex had been seized by the neck, lifted to his feet and jammed against an enormous cedar tree. Three inches off the ground now, his feet twitched uncontrollably. His eyes bulged. Strangling, he was just able to take in the hideous red eyes of the monstrous boy squeezing the life out of him.

The boy, whose sunglasses had been knocked askew, leaned into Dex's face and whispered, "What a coincidence! Maybe it'll be you." But then he said, "Better wait," and dropped Dexter in a heap.

"Yeah, you better wait, you—!" Dex roared, gasping and scrambling to his feet.

Emmet smiled expectantly, but when Dexter failed to finish, he laughed outright. And there was other laughter, too. A tall, lanky boy with upward swept, spiky red hair standing nearby cackled like a lunatic and repeatedly looked back over his shoulder at some other laughing boys behind him. Dex avoided all these well-known hoodlums like the plague. Fortunately, they hadn't been around much that summer—but of course they'd be here now.

"I said keep away!" Emmet yelled at the red haired boy. "Or no deal!"

"All right, all right," the boy said, "C'mon, fellas." Snickering, he led his gang away, looking over his shoulder as he went. Emmet watched them go for a moment, then turned and walked off without another glance at Dex.

But there was still more laughing. Dex saw the rest of them now. Pops, the rich kids who played Frisbee in the park. Dex steered clear of them, too.

It was baffling. Was what happened funny enough to make so many kids who'd otherwise go nowhere near one another stand together and laugh at him this much?

Yes, Dex realized, because he finally felt the wetness spreading down his pant-leg. There were no words to describe the humiliation—or the fury. Dex opened his mouth to rage at these callous jerks, to somehow bring down the sky itself on every last one of them. But he couldn't even manage a word.

Suddenly, thunder exploded directly above. Rain came down in wild sheets, and everyone scattered.

Dex, coming back to his senses, seized the opportunity to slip into the woods and then down onto his hidden trail. Like the living-dead, he shuffled all the way to the Clearing without processing a single thought.

Once there, he walked to the center of the leafy ring and dropped down into a collection of soggy moss and leaves. He could've found a sheltered spot under a tree, but he just didn't care. If there had been a pit dug there, he'd have jumped right in.

For the next hour or so, Dexter lay like a corpse, watching the scene he'd just endured play repeatedly in his mind. *Why couldn't he have said something?* How many times in his life had he prayed for a clever comeback, a razor-sharp word or witty one-liner to demolish a tormenter? He saw other kids do it all the time, but not once had he ever managed it.

Instead, he'd been forced to meet teasing with stone silence, which in its own way was effective. By the end of elementary school, kids stopped asking him to spell words like 'cat' because he simply wouldn't respond. But Dex had always known in his heart-of-hearts that silence was the refuge of the weak.

And now he realized this refuge had been nothing but an illusion, a matter of luck. In avoiding trouble these last few years, he'd also been avoiding the truth. Eventually, Dex now understood, your number comes up. That's when truth grabs you by the throat and makes you piss your pants. It had always been just a matter of time.

Dex tried to fall sleep, but every time he got close, some noise around, some animal rustling or people walking nearby, kept him awake. If someone discovered the Clearing it was going to be the last straw. Mercifully, no one did.

At some point, Dexter thought he heard himself whimpering, but he was sure the wetness sliding down his cheeks was only the rain.

first red, then dead

"I'll be right out," Milton said.

Before Daphna could protest, he disappeared into the cubby, leaving her alone and offended. She'd never been allowed to watch her father actually negotiate the sale of his books because he thought she shouldn't be exposed to the dirty business of haggling. Daphna hadn't minded so much in the past, but recently she'd been reading about the art of negotiation. It was fascinating how many subtle ways there were to get people to agree to your terms. If you were really good, you could even make them feel like they got the better deal.

Instead of heading off to browse, as her indignation urged her to do, Daphna considered something that filled her with guilt. But she had a right, didn't she? Hadn't Milton said a thousand times she'd make a fantastic book scout one day? Well, how was *that* going to happen if she never learned how to bargain?! She was going to be a teenager in a matter of hours, for crying out loud. Besides, he owed it to her for being gone so long.

It was decided.

After glancing over her shoulder, Daphna approached the shelves that composed the cubby's six walls and slowly walked around them. Maybe a little spy hole was already there, so she wouldn't have to make one—not that it would be spying, not really. Technically, maybe, but spying on your father in a used bookstore could hardly be called *real* spying. Daphna felt terrible, there was no denying it, but she was determined.

Unfortunately, there were no spaces visible between the books, and they were all the exact size of the shelves. Daphna ran her finger along the spine of a thick volume, and with the utmost care, pulled at it. She pulled harder. It was stuck. They were all stuck—jammed together like bricks in a wall.

Frustrated, Daphna knelt to tie her shoe. Tugging angrily on the laces, she figured the issue was settled, but from her new position she spotted a book wedged diagonally between two others. After only a moment's hesitation, she leaned forward and peered through the triangular space above it.

By the weak, flickering light of two dripping, misshapen candles, Daphna saw a man who looked like the oldest person in the world. She visited elderly people all the time at Multnomah Village Rest and Rehabilitation Home, the R & R she called it, where she read to a group of senior citizens, but this man looked twice as ancient as most everyone there. Bowed and withered, he had a pasty, pinched face and arms as skinny as twigs.

He wore a brown, featureless robe, in front of which lay a long, snow white beard that shook as his body trembled. Milton

Wax, who was quite a bit older than the parents of Daphna's peers, looked like a tower of strength next to him.

"Give it to me!" the old man suddenly demanded. Milton seemed too stunned to react, as was Daphna. "Give it to me!" he repeated, holding out a skeletal hand. Daphna noticed he had his eyes closed.

"Pardon me?" Milton managed.

Then something even odder happened. For a second Daphna thought she'd gone deaf, because the grizzled buyer mouthed something at her father. However, an instant later she heard him say in a calmer voice, "Give me that book now."

To Daphna's growing surprise and confusion, Milton did exactly that. He set the book on the old man's hand and said, in a perfectly conversational tone, "I've been thoroughly confounded by this book. I'm sure I've never come across anything older. It's filled with nonsense, a hodgepodge of words, most of them not even real as far as

I can tell. I wonder if it's not the journal of a madman or some—"

Daphna knew her father was liable to go on for ages when he started talking about the books he'd acquired. But on this occasion, he'd barely gotten warmed up when the old man clutched the book against his chest and began inhaling and exhaling in deep, raspy gasps.

"Are you okay, Mr.—?" Milton asked, clearly alarmed.

But the old man recovered quickly, though he kept his eyes closed.

"Pardon me," he wheezed. "At my age, a man is prone to bouts of these sorts, but I assure you, I am in no danger." Then he took a deep breath and brought the book back down. "The name's Rash, Asterius Rash."

Daphna knew well that both buyers and sellers cherished unusual volumes, but the way this strange old man cradled Milton's book, the way he lifted and turned it with his knobby knuckles and brought it so close to his face that it touched his forehead—it was like nothing she'd ever seen.

Rash flipped the book over and over, tenderly stroking the mutilated covers with his fingertips and palms; he even passed its cracked spine under his nose, sniffing it like she once saw a man sniff a cigar. Then he put it to his cheek like she'd seen her friends Wren and Teal do with their love notes at school.

Finally, after having done everything but taste it, the old man set the book on the table and rested a hand on it. Was he ever going to open it? He just sat there with his head down and eyes closed, breathing heavily again.

"Mr. Rash?" Milton inquired.

After a moment, Rash's shoulders began to shake. Then his whole frame shuddered as an extended episode of coughing rocked him. The eruptions slowly intensified, coming more and more rapidly in short, throaty bursts. Daphna was sure Rash was having a serious attack, but when the coughing noises transformed into chortles, she realized what was really happening. The old man was laughing. Finally, Rash threw himself back into his chair and roared openly.

No one laughed like that, Daphna thought, and definitely not for this long. Something was seriously wrong with that man. He was even more terrifying than that disgusting boy. She wished her father would excuse himself so they could leave, but Milton just stood there in a perplexed silence, his hands in the pockets of his old tweed blazer.

Daphna's feet were falling asleep. She changed position on her knees, bumping the shelving unit in the process. The noise she made wasn't loud, but Rash abruptly stopped laughing, snapped his eyes open and turned toward the sound. For only an instant, his eyes seemed trained directly on Daphna's peephole, but the instant was more than long enough to make her heart quail beneath her ribs.

It was the eyes again. They weren't red like Emmet's. They were much, much worse.

Rash's eyes were blank, colorless—they were dead. Yet they were also impossibly wide and piercing. Fortunately, they quickly rolled away.

He's blind! Daphna thought. *How can someone appraise books when he can't see them?*

Rash, his interest in the noise apparently gone, had his head back over the book again. He began to speak, this time in a carefully controlled manner. "Please, excuse my little outburst," he said. "This—book, this book of—nonsense—may I ask where you found it?"

Milton didn't respond at first. Then he said, "Perhaps I should come back another time."

Finally! thought Daphna.

"No, my good man," Rash said, smiling. "There is no other time." Then he mouthed something again. Daphna strained to hear, assuming he was whispering, but no, there was nothing. Then Rash said, "Mr. Wax, tell me where you found the book."

Milton responded with no further reluctance. "In a little town in Turkey. Malatya," he said, "in a little shop I'd never realized—"

"Of course you did," Rash sighed, apparently uninterested in the details. He shook his head and smiled as if at an inside joke of some kind. "Of course!" he repeated with a laugh.

Milton looked puzzled, but said, "Is this something you might be interested in?"

"Hmm," Rash considered. "I'm not sure it would be of any use to me, but you've aroused my curiosity."

Daphna nodded. *That's what you're supposed to do,* she thought, *act like you don't really want what you're bargaining for.*

"Let me think a moment," Rash added.

"Certainly," Milton said. While he waited, he twisted his carved silver wedding band around his finger. He always did that with the thumb on the same hand. But he shouldn't be doing that now because it made him look nervous—a major no-no in negotiations. As far as Daphna knew, he hadn't taken the ring off even once in the nearly thirteen years since her mother had died.

Rash seemed deep in thought. He leaned back in his chair and took hold of a long, slender, but cracked, wooden cane resting against the shelf behind him. He laid it on top of his desk, making a slight smack. Daphna realized that must have been the source of the smacking sounds they'd heard in the entry room, but why would he have whacked his desk?

The old man rolled the cane under his hand for a while, then seemed to reach a decision. He mouthed something silently again, after which he said, "You could pay me to take this book from you, but what I need more is some quality help here for a short time. My eyes are no good, and I'm sorry to say the same is now true for my increasingly worthless assistant. Is there any chance you have a bookish youngster at home?"

"My daughter would be delighted to help!" Milton proclaimed, causing Daphna's heart to launch into fearful palpitations. She would be *horrified* to help! And why was her father letting Rash negotiate to *take* the book? Nothing made any sense.

"In fact," Milton continued, making things even worse, "she's out browsing your stacks as we speak! She'd be thrilled to help you now, I'm sure. She loves reading to old folks at the local home," he added, but then he paused and said, "but I do have eight more books to sell at a number of other shops. It's kind of a tradition that we do it together—I've been gone a while, you see—and tomorrow is her thirteenth birthday."

Rash flashed a mouthful of rotten yellow teeth and said, "Tomorrow would be perfect. I promise not to keep her long, and perhaps I'll even find a gift for her here. We open at nine."

"She'll be here," Milton confirmed. Then he asked, "Do we have a deal?"

Daphna blinked, totally baffled. The old man, she realized, hadn't let go of the book for a second. Now he clutched it to his chest again. He mouthed something silently one more time and then said, "You drive a hard bargain, Mr. Wax, but we have a deal. And you can forget all the more curious parts of the exchange we've had here today."

Milton smiled and said, "Outstanding."

Daphna couldn't believe what she was witnessing. *Make him pay for it!* she nearly screamed, but she was upset now about too many things.

She got to her feet and stalked back through the corridors of books feeling drained and disgusted. If that was how her father negotiated, she could understand why she'd never been allowed to watch. With surprising ease given her agitated state, Daphna found her way back to the front desk and lurched outside. Fortunately, that revolting Emmet hadn't returned.

It took a full twenty minutes for Milton to make it out. The moment he stepped through the door, thunder exploded directly above, and rain came down in wild sheets. Daphna and her father fumbled their way into the car as quickly as they could.

Milton started the engine and pulled into to traffic without saying a word, which was fine by Daphna. She watched him out of the corner of her eye as he drove. His brown, speckled eyes were glassy and seemed hardly to blink. Expressions of satisfaction and dis-satisfaction seemed to be fighting for con-trol of his face. It was a depressing sight—he looked like nothing more than a befuddled old man.

Daphna was profoundly disappointed. This had been by far the worst father-daugh-ter bookselling expedition ever. Something awful made her fear that it had also been the last.

everybody today

Daphna was dying to ask questions. She wanted to know how her father could possibly have just given his book away and how Rash could mouth nothing at him and then order him around. But how could she ask anything without giving away the fact she'd spied? It was simple, she couldn't.

The more pressing concern was Rash's request for her help. Milton hadn't said a word about it, and they were nearly home now. Daphna wasn't going to say or do anything to remind him, that was for sure. As they parked in the driveway behind their house, she prepared to hurry to her room.

But just as she put her hand on the door latch, Milton said, "Let's go sell the other books!" He shook his head as if trying to clear the fogginess in his eyes. "I forgot we put them in the trunk! We'll come back for lunch, then grab Dex and Latty and go somewhere fun."

Daphna took a deep breath, then said the unthinkable. "I think I'll take a pass on this one, Dad." She tried her best not to look at her father's face, but she couldn't help it. Just as she feared, a look of wounded disbelief was deforming his already disordered features.

"Ah, you—it—wha—" he stuttered. "But—we—ah—"

Daphna couldn't stand watching her father's face droop like that, so she made up an excuse.

"I really need to write one last letter to Wren and Teal," she said. "They're coming home from camp next week, and the mailman will be here soon."

It wasn't a total lie. She could write a letter. It was just that their note with the camp's address somehow hadn't gotten to her yet.

Eight un-mailed letters sat in her drawer—it might as well be nine. She could give them to the girls when they got home.

Good enough.

Daphna scurried into the house, grateful to find nobody home. She listened for Milton to head off, but he didn't. The car just sat there, idling. Two long minutes crept by before it finally pulled away.

Daphna skulked to her room. She'd spied on her father, then lied to him. It was like she'd become someone else today. She tried to take a nap, but wound up lying in bed, fretting for hours. To ease her conscience, Daphna did write a letter to Wren and Teal, an extra long one, which helped. After that, she managed to sleep, though fitfully.

Just past five, Daphna woke feeling groggy and sapped. She sighed, forced herself out of bed and hurried downstairs, fully expecting to find Latty in a dither.

Latona Pellonia, Latty, was technically Milton's business manager, but she was much more than just that, of course. She was the Wax's housekeeper, nanny, cook, laundress and doer of anything and everything else that needed to get done. But this wasn't always her role. For years, she'd worked for their mother, Shimona, who owned a bookshop in a little town in Israel called Kiryat Shmona. Even though Shimona was Latty's boss, they were best friends.

Everything changed, however, shortly after Shimona met and married Milton and had Dex and Daphna. Shimona retired to raise the twins, but only weeks after they were born, Latty received a tip that books were hidden in some caves in Turkey that could turn the rare book world on its head. Unable to resist, Milton, Shimona and Latty all went.

There was an earthquake.

Milton was seriously hurt when the caves collapsed. He spent weeks in the hospital recovering from multiple bruises and breaks, but that was nothing compared to Shimona. She fell into a chasm and was buried by tons of falling rock. Latty was scarcely hurt at all, at least physically. She stumbled out of the caves under her own power with nothing worse than a host of ugly gashes on her legs, which was lucky because that's why she'd been able to find help. Daphna had no memory of any of this, of course. Neither she nor Dex even remembered living in Israel because they'd moved to Oregon almost immediately after the accident.

Latty's real injuries were emotional. Distraught, she refused to leave the twin's sides afterward, almost literally. She came to Portland and installed herself in the Wax household, which enabled Milton to take over his wife's role as international book scout. She then proceeded to watch over Daphna and Dexter as if they permanently lived inside a cave ready to collapse at any moment.

In the past, Latty's fussing had been bearable to Daphna. It was actually nice to have someone interested in every detail of her life.

But this past year, it had been getting harder and harder to endure. Latty had this increasingly annoying thing about needing to know where she and Dex were at all times. And that's why she was definitely going to be in a dither.

Daphna wasn't sure she could handle Latty just now. She tiptoed into the kitchen and took her seat at the table. Fortunately, Latty was absorbed in preparing her specialty, a Chinese soup called *Min-hun-t'ang*. It was Milton's favorite meal. She'd been out rustling up the ingredients all morning.

When Latty finally turned and saw Daphna, her green eyes panicked. "Daph, you're home!" she cried. "Where's Milton? I checked the computer when I got home and saw he got in earlier, but I assumed he'd come home and taken you kids out. I was just getting worried about why you were late for dinner!"

"We did go out," Daphna sighed. "But Dad dropped me back home. I was safe and sound upstairs taking a nap."

"Yes, but I didn't know that! Where is your father, then? Where's Dex?"

At that moment, Dexter slouched in through the back door looking as dazed as Daphna felt. There were snarls of crumbled leaves in his wet hair and patches of moss clinging to his bedraggled clothes.

"Good Lord, Dexter!" Latty yelped. She was a petite woman, but formidable when worried, which was always. Dex didn't give her the chance to say anything more as he ducked quickly into the laundry room and shut the door.

"You'll catch your death in this weather—with no jacket!" Latty scolded, anyway. "Summer is over! What's going on, Dexter? Why won't you check in these past few days?! I've been worried about you!"

"I fell asleep," Dex said when the door opened again. He came into the kitchen wearing sweats and rubbing his head with a towel.

He wondered when Latty was going to figure out he wasn't about to report his whereabouts to her every five minutes, not any more, anyway. Being a worrywart was her problem, not his.

Dex had considered skipping dinner, even at the risk of Latty calling out the National Guard to search for him, but he knew if he avoided his father much longer, he'd have some serious explaining to do, if he didn't already.

With no further explanation, and without so much as a nod to his sister, Dex sagged into his seat. Daphna was rubbing her eyes and seemed to take no notice of him anyway.

Latty approached the table with a troubled look on her open, pink face, causing both twins to cringe. Even her short frizzled hair looked anxious. "Kids," she said, looking between them, "I know I ask a lot, but I—you know I—"

"—*promised your mother*," Dex and Daphna sighed.

Latty, they knew quite well, had promised their mother that if anything ever happened to her, she'd look after them. The thing was, up until this very moment, the guilt induced by those three words had always worked to bring them into line.

Latty looked alarmed, but the back door opened again.

"Hello, Latona!" Milton called, stepping inside. "Daph told me you were out shopping when I got in."

"Welcome home, Milton!" Latty replied. "Had to get your favorite together. Soup's on!"

But Milton's attention was on Dexter.

"Hello, Dex!" he said, clapping Dexter on the shoulder in an extravagantly fatherly sort of way. He was overdoing it by a long shot, Daphna thought, probably because he wasn't sure how to approach his son after being so rudely blown off. She felt a stab of irritation with her brother for making what should be a simple hello so complicated.

Dex wasn't quite sure what to make of the greeting. It seemed phony. Milton Wax wasn't one of those touchy-feely, I-love-you blubbering kind of dads, which was something Dex actually appreciated.

"Hey, Dad," he replied, trying to sound totally bored.

"Hey, what'd you get for the rest of the books?" Daphna asked, annoyed by her brother's needlessly indifferent tone.

"Well," Milton answered, tucking himself into his place at the table, "Sold a nice copy of Yeats' *Nineteen Hundred and Nineteen*." Then he smiled and said, "And I did drive a hard bargain over at that new place, your ABC."

Daphna looked at her father incredulously, but then his still glassy eyes fluttered a bit, and his face fell.

"You look exhausted, Milton!" Latty cried, setting down the tureen of soup. "Why didn't you come right in to rest? What is wrong with everybody today?"

"I'm fine, Latona," Milton replied, but rather unconvincingly. "I'm a bit tired, I suppose. Perhaps I'll turn in early this evening."

"Perhaps definitely. Eat up and go have a hot soak. Then straight to bed."

Milton didn't argue. Instead he said, "Oh, Daph, speaking of that new place, the old bookbuyer, Mr. Rash, he'd like you to stop by tomorrow morning to lend a hand, or your eyes, as it turns—"

"*Rash?!*" Latty looked horrified. "His name is Rash? That's—What an *awful* name."

"Why *me?!*" Daphna demanded. "It's not fair with all the reading I do at the R & R!" Which reminded her, "And I'm already supposed to go there tomorrow! Make Dex!"

"He wouldn't want me," Dex said, scowling at his sister. "And anyway, valuable books always fall to pieces if I even look at them. You can't rely on anything old if you ask me."

It seemed to Daphna that this last comment was directed toward their father, but maybe she was just imagining her brother's peevishness. He'd damaged a small library full of fragile books before he quit having anything to do with their father's livelihood. Whatever the case, Milton didn't seem to notice Dex's comment.

What Milton *did* notice was Daphna. He stared fixedly at her, his forehead creased with consternation.

"Mr. Rash merely requires some assistance," he said. "He's blind and needs some sharp eyes."

"But why *my* eyes?" Daphna complained, wondering at her father's oddly *un*-sharp eyes and rather monotone explanation.

"Don't you want to learn how the place really works, especially after all the time you've spent there this summer?"

"Where I spend my free time is up to me!" Daphna roared, surprised at her own anger. "It's not my fault Wren and Teal get to go to camp while I'm stuck around here all day with nothing to do! And I wouldn't even know if a friend called me since Dexter can't be bothered to write down a message!"

To Dex, his sister's reaction to a perfectly reasonable comment seemed excessive. She was losing it, and the whole thing was, frankly, quite entertaining. She was probably just embarrassed about spending her summer days in a bookstore—she should be anyway.

"If anyone ever called you," he cracked, "I'd call the six o'clock news."

"Oh, shut up, Dexter!"

"Daphna," said Milton.

"*Dad*, you *gave* him that book *for free!*"

Daphna bit her tongue. She'd just admitted that she'd been spying.

In response, Milton only blinked at her. He looked startled, but also much more lucid. But then he exploded. "Damn it, Daphna!" he hollered, "You'll go because I said so! Nine a.m. sharp. Tomorrow morning!"

Tears shot to Daphna's eyes. She turned

to look for help from Latty, but she wasn't in the kitchen anymore. Daphna hadn't even seen her leave. She was at a loss. This was absolutely not Milton Wax. Milton Wax did not yell. Milton Wax did not swear. Milton Wax had never once in his life as a parent uttered the words, 'Because I said so,' to either of his children, in any tone of voice.

Even he seemed to recognize the unprecedented nature of this eruption. His mouth was open. His lips were quivering. "I—I'm—" he stuttered.

Daphna didn't give her father the chance to apologize. She sprinted from the room.

"Dexter," Milton said, turning to him when she'd gone, "you'll go along, too. It won't kill you to help your sister this one time."

Dex glared at his father. He was only doing this so Daphna wouldn't think she was being picked on alone! Dexter refused to melt down, though, even if his father had scared him, too. Dex wanted to lash out, to tell his father to take a flying leap, but he couldn't do it. The words just wouldn't come.

"Whatever," Dex managed in a slightly tremulous voice.

He got up and walked out of the room, wondering if even a shred of dignity was left to his name.

some fun

It wasn't even six o'clock, but both Wax children were in their beds. Daphna burst into sobs the second she reached her room and cried for nearly fifteen minutes. She wished her father would just go away again if this was how he was going to be when he came home.

There was one good thing about her fit, though. It wiped her out. As soon as it was over, Daphna fell headlong into deep, dreamless sleep.

Dexter had no such luck. If he was falling headlong into anything, it was despair. He collapsed on his bed and lay there simmering for hours. There was no way he was going to that bookstore. He knew his sister.

At some point, she'd ask if she could poke around and try to make him help the old man, whoever he was, probably in the name of "fairness," which seemed to be her favorite word sometimes—like she knew the first thing about what was fair and unfair. And now even mild-mannered Milton Wax was getting aggressive and telling him what to do! The tension burned inside until he felt ready to combust.

At one a.m., Dexter decided enough was enough. He went upstairs and hurried past Latty's room to his father's door. He was going to tell Milton Wax to take that flying leap.

Dex took a deep breath, then softly pushed the door open.

"*I'm failing. I know it,*" his father whispered.

This simple statement sent a torrent of relief through Dex's clenched muscles. At once, all desire to condemn his father faded away. "No, Dad, I—I—"

"*It's all wrong. I can feel it,*" Milton moaned.

Dex didn't respond this time because his father wasn't talking to him. He was talking to himself, in his sleep.

The streetlight outside threw enough light into the room to make the portrait of Dex's mother visible, so he pondered her thoughtful, oval face for a moment. It was something he rarely ever did, even though there were pictures of her all over the house.

She had petite features like Latty. They kind of looked alike, except his mother had long, flowing hair and bluish eyes. She was pretty, and despite the deep worry lines spreading out over her brow and from the corners of her mouth, she looked happy. Fatigued, but happy. She'd been somewhere near fifty when Dex and Daphna were born, which he knew was really late in life to have kids.

"*I'm botching it,*" Milton whined, startling Dex from his contemplation. "*I know* it," he added. "*I—I—I can't quite—I'm just not sure—I am not a bad man.*" A horrible sound, a wretched lament of some sort, escaped his throat.

Dex remained silent, simply watching as his father continued to mutter. Finally, he walked out of the room and headed back downstairs. He hurled himself on his bed and stayed there for the rest of the night, dipping in and out of a corrosive, embittered sleep.

At breakfast, Latty set two bowls of bite-sized, choke-proof mixed fruit on the table next to a cereal box and then informed the twins that their father had left an hour earlier on a local book scouting venture. He'd gotten wind of two high-end estate sales, which were often goldmines for rare books. She said he might be gone for most of the day. Then she said she had some errands to run.

The twins both sensed something was off. Latty sounded even more nervous than normal.

"Promise you'll leave a note if you go anywhere," Latty insisted, wrapping herself in a shawl at the door. Neither of the twins responded. Neither was in the mood. "Please," Latty said, nearly begging. "Just for my peace of mind."

Dex rolled his eyes.

"Dexter," Latty asked softly, "Why is this so—?"

"We're not babies," Daphna declared. Normally it was easier just to promise, but right now she simply didn't feel like it.

"I know you're not babies," Latty assured the twins. "It's just that every time you two leave my sight, I'm certain something awful is going to happen to you. *Please*—it's more for me than you."

"No," was Dexter's adamant response.

"Okay," Daphna conceded. Latty's eyes had dialed directly into panic mode.

Dex snorted.

"Thank you, dear," Latty said to Daphna. Then she looked at Dex. "You don't want me wandering around all day looking for you, do you, Dex?"

"FINE!" Dex shouted. "I'll call you every eight steps I take, *okay?!*"

Latty looked uncertain how to reply to this. She decided on, "Thank you, but every few hours would do nicely."

But then she added, to Daphna, "Oh, listen, I know your father asked you to go to that bookshop to help Mr. Rash, but I realized this morning why his name upset me so much last night. Book scouting is a small world. Your mother and I knew an Asterius Rash, a long time ago. He is a dishonest businessman and a notoriously unstable character.

"I didn't get a chance to speak to your dad about it this morning, but I'm sure he'd agree that it's best you don't go. In fact, Daphna, I'd seriously think about staying away from that place altogether. I know you think I worry about you too much, but in this case, actually, I insist because, like I said—"

"Sure!" Daphna said. "I understand.

Thanks for looking out for me."

Latty grinned, obviously surprised. Then she said, "Go have some fun. It's your birthday, isn't it?" Then she winked, turned, and left with a bit of a jump in her step.

"That does it," Dex spat, spiking his spoon on the table. He'd been planning to wait for his father to announce the grand birthday plan so he could flat-out refuse to go along.

"But he mentioned my birthday yesterday to that old man!" Daphna protested. "And Latty just—"

"So?" Dex sneered. "He probably forgot the second he heard about these stupid sales. Latty's going out to get presents right now so she can hide them under his bed. You know it!"

Before Daphna could respond, the phone rang. She grabbed it with a snarl, but brightened up when she heard her father's voice. Surely, he'd have something big to announce. Maybe the estate sales were a ruse.

Instead, Milton said, "Hi, Daph. I just wanted to make sure you won't be late for your appointment with Mr. Rash."

"Oh, Dad," said Daphna, "Latty just told us we can't go. She remembered him from when she used to work with Mom. She said he's nuts or something."

"She what?" Milton replied. "No, she must have him confused with someone else. He was totally professional yesterday."

"*What?*"

"Daphna," Milton said, "I told him you'd be there. You know a scout's reputation is his biggest asset. I've got to run," he abruptly concluded. Then he hung up.

Daphna jammed the phone down. "*What?*" she demanded when she saw the smirk on Dexter's face.

"Going then?"

"You're supposed to come, too, Dexter," Daphna retorted. "I heard Dad last night, so don't act like you don't know anything about it. It's not like I really want you to go, you know. I know you'd rather die than set foot in a bookstore, but I really am creeped out by that Rash guy, not to mention that sicko, Emmet, who works in the front of the store. Some really weird things happened there yesterday. You have no idea. He's—"

"Sorry," Dex interrupted, "I've got other plans."

"No you don't! You're just going to mess around in the park all day!"

"I'm meeting my French tutor," Dex said. "Forgot to mention that yesterday."

Oh, Daphna was hot now.

"Dexter," she fumed, "I know you lied about getting a tutor to get Latty off your back! I'm not an idiot!"

"Says who?" Dex growled.

"You're the one that failed French!"

So Daphna knew about that. His first 'F'. Scraping by had been getting harder and harder with all the newfangled "On-demand, Performance" tests in middle school.

"Mind your own business," was the best

Dex could come up with.

"Love to," Daphna replied. "What do I care if you want to screw up your life?"

"And what do I care if you have no life to screw up?" countered Dex. Boy, did that feel good. "It's classic that you turned into a book freak," he added, getting going, "and now Dad doesn't care about you anymore, either. Who's not an idiot now?"

"That's not true!"

"Daphna," said Dex, "he cares more about books than his own kids' birthday! It's not like he ever makes any money scouting! You know we have enough from Mom to get by."

Daphna ground her teeth. She was being worn down, and surprisingly quickly.

"Fine," she said, "go wherever it is you go!" Before Dex could reply, she added, "But I really would avoid *France* if I were you."

Dex leaned across the table and laced his sister with the most hostile glare he could manage. To his horror, she not only met, but held, his gaze. It took effort, but he stood up calmly, got his sweatshirt from the laundry room and then opened the back door.

"*Au revoir*," Dex said, and he was gone.

aloft and amazed

Steaming, Daphna put the breakfast dishes into the sink—Dexter's too, of course—then reluctantly headed out the door for the ABC.

As she walked under the morning's overcast sky, Daphna couldn't help but think about her father. Not a bit of what Dexter said was true. He was just trying to be cruel. Dex was probably as smart as she was, smarter when it came to remembering exact details, if he cared about them, that is. But he was simply never going to get it together until he started actually *wanting* to. How complicated of a concept was that?

Daphna tried to elbow what Dex said out of her mind, but the words gnawed at her. The fact was she was furious if their dad really did forget their birthday. Maybe there was something to part of what Dex had said, but she wasn't going to wrack her brains to figure out how much and which part. And that crack about her having no life! *What a jerk!*

She had lots of friends at school. Practically every day people sought her out, even Pops! Daphna doubted there was anyone in her entire grade who didn't know who she was, while hardly a soul knew Dexter Wax existed. It was Dexter who had no clue how to make friends. Wren and Teal were Pops, and two of the biggest! So what if she never spent time with them after school?

Daphna wasn't silly enough to think she was a Pop. She could never be as pretty and stylish and sophisticated as any of them, even if she sometimes thought she looked a bit like Teal. But Wren and Teal were still her *friends*. Anyway, she had too much homework in the Talented and Gifted classes to hang out after school. If Wren and Teal had been around this summer, she'd have seen them once in a while. All of this was so upsetting that Daphna completely forgot about Rash until she opened the front door of the shop.

Emmet was at the desk. When he looked up and fixed her with those red, ruined eyes, Daphna felt like screaming again. Instead she marched right up to Emmet with her hand extended. He gaped at it like he'd never seen a hand before, then, tentatively held out his own.

"We weren't formally introduced yesterday," Daphna said. "I'm Daphna Wax."

"Ah—um—"

"You're Emmet."

"Yeah."

"I'm glad to know you, Emmet. I guess I'm helping out your boss today for a short while. I think I'm late, so I'll just head on back." Daphna took her hand back and left Emmet staring dumbly at his own. Then, with an exhale she hoped wasn't obvious, turned and entered a hall of books, heading for Rash's cubby, planning to get this over with as fast as humanly possible.

Dex saw his sister go in. Curiosity about this Rash character had gotten the best of him on the way to the Clearing.

When he'd approached the shop and seen Emmet inside, the shock sent him fleeing into an alley across the street. Dex had thought about warning Daphna when she got there, but decided against it. She seemed to know about him anyway, and maybe a little justice could be served. Maybe she'd get a bit of what he'd gotten yesterday.

But now that he'd seen her go inside, Dex felt apprehensive. The last thing he wanted was to go in there. He'd rather see the place go up in flames. But if something did happen to Daphna, he'd somehow get blamed for not going with her, he was sure of it.

Dex hesitated a moment longer, then hit

upon on a compromise. He'd go over and try to peek in a bit further. Maybe he could catch his sister doing something embarrassing for the old man, or maybe he could learn something humiliating about Emmet in case they ever crossed paths again.

Dex slipped out of the alley, then crossed the street out of sight of the ABC. He obviously couldn't just waltz right in, so he hurried down a flight of concrete steps that led behind the building.

The old warehouse sat on a grass and gravel covered slope above a row of stores along a busy road below. There were no rear entrances; the back face of the building didn't have a single window or door. It was just a giant, ugly wall of peeling wood planks.

Defeated already, Dex slumped against it. Torrents of frustration coursed through his body. It was a feeling Dex knew well, and as usual, he didn't know how to deal with it.

Enough was enough. Dex needed to go to the Clearing. He turned to leave, but as he did, a giant drop of cold rain fell directly on his head. Dex looked up, unreasonably furious. Rain was dripping off the edge of the warehouse's roof.

The roof!

Dex walked along the wall, searching for a way to climb on top of the store. Lo and behold, on the far side of the building was a rusty ladder. How could he have given up before walking around the whole place?

Carefully, Dex climbed the slick ladder and stepped onto the wide, flat roof. Just at his feet was a small, square, downward-facing door. "Trapdoor!" Dex whispered. The very idea of a trapdoor was exciting, even if there was probably one on top of every warehouse on the planet. The only problem was that this one had a rusty lock on it.

Breathing deeply, Dex knelt down and lifted the lock, and he was rewarded for keeping his composure. The lock simply broke right off the door when he gave it the slightest pull. Pleased, Dex lifted the door and laid it over onto the roof. Then he peered into the opening—and almost total darkness.

Dex had to think a moment. There had to be more than one floor, or a loft for storage. *Perfect*, he thought, lowering his face into the hole. The smell of rotting wood wafted up and almost choked him, but he got a glimpse of another ladder mounted on the wall leading between the trapdoor and the floor below.

Dex took another deep breath and climbed down onto the ladder. The first step was fine, but he heard an ominous creak when he put his foot on the second rung. The ladder pulled the slightest bit away from the wall, causing his heart to drop into his stomach. Holding perfectly still, Dex considered how wise this little mission was. Then he decided he didn't care. He lowered his other foot and the ladder seemed to hold. Slowly, he descended into the blackness below.

One foot after another. *This isn't so bad*, Dex thought, at least until he heard the long, pained creak of protest made by the planking at the bottom of the ladder. Instinctively, he squatted, but got a nose full of dust and decay for his effort. Nearly choking again, Dex looked up for something to provide direction. There was something, straight ahead—a dim line of light cut across the warehouse. He was on a loft, and it ended somewhere ahead. If he could make his way to the edge, he'd probably have no problem seeing down into the store.

Any thoughts of turning back ceased. However unsafe, however scary, Dex was having fun. It was as simple as that. He couldn't remember the last time he'd been so plainly *interested* in doing something.

Dex began to crawl. The floor was rotting. He could dig his nails into it easily, but he still moved swftly. But then, after a good twenty or thirty feet, a loud crack sounded under his left hand. Dex froze, worried someone might've heard him and half expecting to fall right through the floor to his death.

Dexter held his breath and waited a long minute, then leaned forward until he was lying flat on his stomach. From this position, he began sliding forward, almost swimming through the heaps of dust. This disgusting method seemed to be the answer, and Dex worked his way toward the sliver of light ahead, breathing as little as possible.

Finally, he reached the edge and looked over.

What Dexter saw was a labyrinth. The flat tops of hundreds of shelving units spread across his field of vision in interlocking hexagons of varying size. It was momentarily mesmerizing. But then, running his eyes along the edge of the loft, Dex noticed he'd somehow crawled toward the far end of the store, and the moment he realized this, a noise—someone humming to herself—drew his attention directly down. A woman was there, browsing.

When Dex's eyes adjusted to the weak light around her, he gasped. He knew that thick head of snow-white hair and those broad shoulders. It was Ruby, his secret friend. She looked up when he gasped, and to Dex it seemed she was staring right at him, though her face showed no sign of recognition. He must be hidden by the shadows of the loft. Could she see him or not? Should he roll away? Then, another noise.

Ruby turned her attention away. Emmet was there now, too. The pair looked at each other, but did not speak. It was downright weird watching them face one another so impassively. Finally, Emmet simply walked away.

Confused, Dex decided to make his way along the loft's edge to follow Emmet, but it was difficult since he could only move along the center of the store, and very slowly at that. Dex lost sight of Emmet almost right away, but at some point near the middle of the warehouse, he heard another voice, Daphna's, coming from just ahead.

"But *why*?" she was asking, sounding distressed.

Dex hurried through the dust until he thought he was right above her. Yes, she was there, sitting at a desk inside a tiny candle-lit room walled in by very high, tightly packed shelves. Across from Daphna sat an old geezer with a brown robe and white beard. He was leaning forward, gripping a long, skinny book lying open in front of his sister.

"Mr. Rash?" she asked.

After a moment, the old man responded in a painfully hoarse voice. "Excuse me, my dear. I was distracted for a moment. Something going on in the back of the store. We must always be vigilant about—thieves."

"But, how do you know what's going on in the back of the store?"

"I have acute hearing, something that develops when one's eyes fail. Please, read it again."

Dex was forced to doubt what he'd just heard. How could the old man have known what was going on so far back there, especially when no one said a word?

"I don't mean to be rude, Mr. Rash, but why?" Daphna asked again. "I've read the same thing who knows how many times now, and I've stared at this page for so long, my eyes are crossing. Wouldn't you like me to read on?"

In response, Rash mumbled something that sounded like "Graaal." Then he said, "Read me the passage one more time," in a way that reminded Dex of teachers.

Without further protest, Daphna took a deep breath, then began to read, but Rash didn't sit back to listen. Instead, he remained leaning forward, gripping the sides of the long book as if he feared Daphna might grab it and run.

He must really be paranoid, Dex thought, scoffing at the thought of his sister even contemplating swiping the book—the girl who freaks out if a library book is five minutes overdue, the girl who freaks out if someone *else's* library book is five minutes overdue.

"Sutro," Daphna read, "ibn lanik exos nada—"

"*What was that?!*" Rash interrupted, reacting as if Daphna had just sworn at him in Swahili or something. Maybe she had. Dex hadn't the slightest idea what she'd just read. It sounded like gibberish.

"*What?!*" Rash demanded again. "Did you say exos nada? *Did you, girl?!*"

"Oh, sorry," Daphna hurriedly replied. "Nadas. It says, 'Exo nadas.' I read it wrong that time. Is it important?"

Rash gave out with a fantastically wearied sigh. "More than you could possibly know, my dear," he said. "Please, begin again."

"Sutro," Daphna repeated, this time very deliberately. "Ibn lanik exo nadas circa earl."

Dex shook his head. Not a word of that made sense. And it was definitely not English.

"Should I go on, Mr. Rash?" Daphna asked.

"Marvelous! Marvelous!" the old man croaked. "Don't you agree? Such promise these words possess! There is no need to go on right now," Rash said. Then he added, "Good things come to those who wait, child. Don't let anyone ever tell you to ignore clichés."

"Ah—," Daphna said, but Rash wasn't finished.

"If I may advise," he continued, "don't fight Fate, my dear. You need simply wait." Rash laughed a long, satisfied chortle at his felicitous turn of phrase.

"What do you mean?" Daphna asked. "I don't understand."

"What I am saying, young lady, is that in the infinity of Time, all things must come to pass. In some future time, you and your father will come to my store, but we will not meet. In another, you will not come at all. In still another, you will bring me a book that only closely resembles the book I seek, and I will be disappointed. All of this must be in the fullness of Time.

"But, you see, *this* time, Daphna, your father brought me *this* book, and then he gave me you, too. If this book is what I believe it is, and if I believed in luck, I'd say yesterday was the luckiest day of a long and unlucky life."

"I—I'm still not sure I—"

"Not to worry!" Rash replied. "Not to worry! Let me chat with you a moment. Tell me about your family."

"Well," Daphna said, sounding relieved not to have to read the strange line yet again, "you met my father. He's a book scout, obviously. It used to be a hobby, but he's been doing it pretty much full time lately, I guess. My mom was a scout, too, but she died when I was a baby."

"I'm sorry to hear that," Rash said, though to Dex's ear he didn't sound the least bit sorry.

"Yeah. We never knew her," Daphna continued. "My father doesn't talk much about her. She died in Turkey, in an accident right after we were born. She was a book scout first, actually. He came into her store one day. He's got pictures of her up everywhere. I can't stand that one in the living room. It takes up the entire mantle. I never invite friends over 'cause I don't want them to see it. They'll look at me funny. Their moms are beautiful and—young, and alive, of course."

"You have her eyes," Rash said, startling both twins. "I knew your mother long before she married your father," he explained. "In another lifetime, you might say. Your father must be a genuine romantic to have won such an extraordinary woman. Oh, Time, thy pyramids!"

"A romantic," Daphna laughed. "That's a good one."

"Tell me about your brother, the wanderer with sharp hair. He shares your mother's eyes."

"He's my twin," Daphna said, "but we're nothing alike—I can promise you that. His name is Dexter."

Dex was confused. How could the old man know what he looked like if he couldn't see? How could he know what Daphna looked like for that matter? Emmet must have told him.

"Perhaps I should meet the boy," Rash mused.

"I don't know," said Daphna. "You'd have a hard time getting him to step foot in here. He's one of those kids who doesn't think much, like he'll just be ready for whatever life has in store—no need to study, no need to be serious about anything. I don't think he's ever seen a comb or tucked in a shirt since the day he was born. It's like he doesn't care what the world thinks of him.

"I try to help him out, but he just won't listen to me, or anyone really. I'm not sure what he thinks he's going to do with his life. Though he's really good at some things. I can never fool him because he always remembers exactly what I say."

"How disappointing. I'm so glad to see you've chosen a wiser path."

Dex seized up with rage. He wanted to throw heavy objects over the edge of the loft. He wanted to scream out that Daphna was a nerd and a loser and the biggest snob in the history of the world. The only reason he managed to restrain himself was that he was stunned to hear his sister speaking so freely with a stranger. She was a private person, and not given to rambling like that, even on subjects she was well practiced in—like insulting him.

Dex was incensed enough, though. He slid around and prepared to make his way back toward the ladder. But he paused when Rash said, "Now, this won't hurt a bit."

"What?" Daphna asked, tension infusing her voice. "What won't hurt a bit?"

Rash laughed. "I'm going to say something. Your eyes may itch, but it won't hurt."

"My eyes?"

Rash didn't respond. He appeared to be

concentrating.

"Did you say my eyes are going to itch?" Daphna asked again.

"Quiet!" Rash ordered. "I'm trying to remember."

"But—!"

"Silence!"

Daphna, apparently cowed, did not speak again.

"Blast it!" Rash cried. "After so much planning, how could I forget to check that word?! Blast my fading memory! But no matter," he said, now in a tone that suggested he was talking to himself. "I'll need to consult my ledger—of course that could take all night with that ineffectual fool. Should I keep you here? What's the point?! What's one more day?!"

Then he laughed and shouted something that sounded like "Kalice!" There was silence for a moment, then Rash leaned forward and said, "Daphna, dear, listen closely—"

"Yes?" Daphna asked, and quite meekly.

"Thank you for reading to me from my book about birds. You will return tomorrow morning. We will finish what we've started here and then leave shortly after. You will be, as you wish so desperately to be, *my new assistant*. If all goes well, we'll begin watching for the First Tongue immediately."

"Oh, thank you, Mr. Rash!" was Daphna's enthusiastic reply.

Dex was stupefied. Did she not understand that he just told her they'd be *leaving*? What did she think she was doing? He'd seen enough. Dex got to his knees and crawled with relative speed back across the loft, too aggravated to worry about his safety anymore. The boards groaned beneath him, but did not give way, and he was quickly back on the ladder, which only moved a hair when he climbed it.

Dexter scrambled onto the roof, hurried down to the ground and around the building, and in no time at all was back in the alley across the street.

He didn't head off though, but rather just stood there, trying to sort out what he'd seen.

He was still standing there ten minutes later when Daphna finally came out of the ABC. She rubbed her eyes at the dismal, gray day.

recovered memory

Daphna looked around. She'd somehow forgotten where she was and what she was doing, and the feeling was frightening.

Dex watched her standing there, looking as if she'd just woken up somewhere she hadn't gone to sleep. Her bewildered expression was comical. He was glad he hadn't taken off because he suddenly decided to find out what Daphna was up to. He'd always suspected that her good-girl routine was a fraud—or at least he'd found himself often hoping so. And now it might actually turn out to be true. Besides, all the spying he'd managed had galvanized him in a way he'd never been before.

"Hey!" he called, brushing and whacking at the dust clinging all over him.

Daphna saw him and crossed the street hesitantly. The pair walked half a block to the village coffee shop and sat down at a table in front with a green umbrella attached.

Daphna was still mired in confusion, but she finally looked at her brother. "You're all dusty," she said.

Brushing himself again, Dex said, "So you met this Rash guy then, huh?"

Daphna screwed up her eyes for a moment. It looked to Dex like she thought he was the one talking gibberish. "Oh, Mr. Rash!" she finally realized. "He's okay. I was just being silly—I guess."

"Hmm, interesting," Dex said, tingling with anticipation. Daphna was going to lie to him. "So, you two just hung out, chatted and whatnot. A nice, friendly old man."

"Well, yeah. I guess so."

"What did you talk about?" Toying with his sister was fun, a rare opportunity.

"We didn't talk all that much—I guess. We went to his little cubby, and I read him something—a book about—birds."

"Birds, huh?"

"Yeah, birds. I guess he's some kind of bird-lover or something. I'm going back tomorrow to finish it."

As much as Dex enjoyed the idea of stringing his sister along, he suddenly lost patience. "Just how stupid do you think I am, Daphna? I've always known you were a phony."

"What do you mean, phony? Who called you stupid? But never mind, you're being stupid now."

Dex tried to calm himself. Of course Daphna couldn't know he was on to her.

"Okay, tell me this," he said. "Did you talk about me?"

"*Oh, sure*, we talked about you the whole time. I mean, as you know, the world revolves around you." But Daphna looked deeply uncertain, however pointed her words.

"So," Dex continued, relishing the upper hand, "there was no time to squeeze in anything about Mom and Dad then?"

"What, like I'm going to tell a complete stranger the story of my life? *I'm* not stupid, you know." Daphna was getting angry now. Her brother was obviously looking for some way to put her down. He constantly made fun of her for visiting the old folks at The R & R.

Dex and Daphna turned away from each other, exasperated, and both happened to look over at the ABC. Emmet was out front, donning his shades and heading off to do who knew what awful things.

"I just don't see why you need some old fart to get you out of here," Dexter said. "If you want to run away, just run away."

"I have no idea what you're talking about, Dexter," Daphna retorted. "Is this your idea of a joke?" She got to her feet. "I don't know why I even bother," she said, "but here's a little piece of advice: people might actually talk to you if you learned some basic social skills."

"You mean like they talk to you?"

"Yes!"

"Daphna," Dex said, amazed. He'd often considered saying this, but now was the time, after what she said about him to Rash. "Are you telling me," he sneered, "that you don't know the only time anyone talks to you at school is so you'll do their work?"

"YOU'RE A BIG FAT LIAR, DEXTER WAX!" Daphna wailed. "Wren and Teal—"

"I saw them both in the park last week," Dex said. He laughed. This was a bald-faced lie, but if he had to hear his sister say those two names one more time, he was going to lose his mind.

"I don't believe you," Daphna muttered, her voice broken.

Deciding he'd won, Dex looked at his sister and said, coolly, "Daphna, you know very well you weren't reading a book about birds. You were sitting across from that old dude, and he was making you read some gobbledygook over and over in a long, skinny book—he was leaning over, holding on to it while you read, like you were gonna eat the pages or something."

Daphna screwed up her whole face. Her mind was twisting. Why was Dex saying these things, and why did they make her feel so dizzy?

"And he said some wacko words," Dex added, smirking. In a magician's extravagant voice and with an exaggerated flourish of his hands, he pronounced, "Graaaal!"

"*That's right!*" Daphna's face had drained itself of color, and she tottered on her feet. It all started coming back in a rush.

"That's right!" she repeated, falling back into her chair and breaking into tears. "I—I was so scared!" she sputtered. "Dex! How—how do you know this?!"

Dex scrutinized his sister. She was nearly hyperventilating. She looked frantic, really scared, and—he had to admit—she was no actress.

So he told her he'd happened to see Emmet go into the store, and since he'd seen him around the neighborhood menacing people, he'd decided to spy on him, which led to his discovery of the rusted trap door on the roof leading to the loft overhanging half the warehouse. It was a weak story, he knew, but Daphna was in no condition to dissect it.

Daphna shivered as Dexter spoke, her very bones recalling the terror she suppressed the whole time she sat in Rash's creepy little cubby. It was a much more powerful version of what she'd felt upon seeing his silhouette through the curtain with her father. She couldn't conceive of how she hadn't remembered any of it.

"I'll never go near him again!" Daphna swore. "Why did he make me keep reading that—that—what was it, Dex?"

"I have no idea," said Dex. "It made no sense. He said you were going to be his new assistant."

"He wants me to leave with him!" Daphna wailed. She was appalled. "Who is he? Why does he want me?"

Dex disliked the look that passed momentarily across his sister's face. It was as if she'd pondered which of her outstanding qualities made her so abductable.

"He said something about watching for the First Tongue right away," Dex said, letting it go. "But that makes no sense."

This was something to latch on to at least. Unnerved at the thought of being kidnapped, Daphna considered the phrase a moment.

"Well," she said, "'Tongue' can also mean language, of course. I'm tutoring in both French and Spanish this year. But what could 'first language' mean?"

"Who knows?" Dex replied, irritated by his sister's know-it-all tone. But then, mostly kidding, he said, "Once on TV, I saw some guy hypnotize his dog by chanting some goofy word. Made him think he was a duck, and he actually started quacking."

"Yes!" Daphna cried. "It has to be something like that! Wait, if Rash thinks it's some kind of magic language, then of course he'd be interested in it! That whole place has nothing but books on magic!" She put her heels on the edge of the chair and wrapped her arms around her knees.

"Is it possible?" Daphna asked. "He scares me, Dex. When he talks, all you know is his voice. I was in a daze. Something freaky is going on. I don't think I would ever have remembered if you hadn't—"

"—told you what happened."

Daphna leapt to her feet. "Wait a minute! He made Dad give him that book yesterday. He was doing some weird thing moving his lips, but he must have hypnotized Dad, too! At dinner, Dad started to remember when I told him he gave the book away! I didn't tell him enough!"

"Dad's mixed up in all this." Dex realized it the moment he said it.

"Why do you say that?!" Daphna demanded.

Dex told her how he'd found their father

in the middle of the night muttering about "botching" things and how he wasn't a "bad man."

"Well," Daphna replied, taking her seat once again, "maybe that's because he didn't mean to give a potentially valuable book away to such a psycho. He did botch the negotiation for it, but that's because Rash made him! Maybe he said he's not a bad man because he feels guilty for staying away on this last scouting trip for so long! *Who knows?* We've got to find him and tell him what happened!"

"That wasn't the only word he said," Dex realized. He was warming up to the idea that Rash really was some sort of hypnotist. "He also said, 'Kalice.'"

"This is crazy," Daphna said, "but something tells me I'm lucky to have gotten out of there." She looked down at the tabletop and said, "About all that stuff I said about you—well, I'm sorry. It's just that if you actually took it as advice, you'd—"

Dex looked blankly at his sister. One of her classic "apologies." It didn't even deserve a response.

"Anyway," Daphna said, "I'm going home to wait for Dad to come back. Hey! Maybe that's what that book is! It was full of bizarre looking words! Maybe they're for hypnotism!"

"What was he going to do to your eyes?" Dex asked, wondering if such a thing might actually be possible.

"I don't know," Daphna said. "But he said he needed something in that ledger Emmet always has up front. Anyway," she said again, shuddering, "I don't care. I'm never going anywhere near either one of those horrid people again for as long as I live."

"You know," Dex said, "that guy who made his dog start quacking. He had to say his word again to make it stop."

"Right! Maybe we can snap Dad out of it with those words! What were they again?"

"'Graal' and 'Kalice.'"

"Graal and Kalice, Graal and Kalice," Daphna repeated. Then she leveled her eyes at Dex and said, "You're a duck."

"What? Oh, quack," Dex said with the hint of a smile.

"Worth a try," Daphna said, smiling too. But then she got serious again. "Maybe we don't have the words just right, but they really are worth a try." She rose again and said, "We both should go home and wait for Dad. Latty's probably already having a conniption."

"You go," said Dex. "I'm gonna hang out for a while, do some thinking."

"Ah, okay," Daphna replied, though she wanted to slug Dexter for his total lack of concern for their father. But the truth was she'd probably be better off without his help.

She headed off, muttering, "Graal and Kalice. Graal and Kalice," as she walked.

Dex had no intentions of thinking. *Doing* was his new thing. He got up, made sure Emmet wasn't around, then rushed across the street and back down behind the warehouse.

Daphna, for once, had given him a good idea. If this were true, if it wasn't just TV gimmicks combined with his sister going crazy, and there really were words that could hypnotize people—even though it went against every fiber of his being, against his bottomless loathing of books and everything to do with them—he wanted those words. Ruby would help him. She was good at languages, his French grade notwithstanding. *Even just one, if it's the right one*, Dex thought, *my life would never be the same.*

Dexter climbed to the roof and back down onto the loft with no problems. As he forced his way through the dust toward Rash's cubby, he realized this was actually turning out to be the best day he'd had in recent memory, even if it involved his sister. Then he was there, and Rash was right below him, sitting at his desk.

"Calm yourself, Asterius," Rash exhorted himself while leafing tenderly through the pages of the book. His voice was nearly hysterical. "You can't be certain. Don't be hasty this time! Emmet, you fool! This is no time for your ridiculous hunting! Bring me my ledger! Blast my memory!" Rash went back to fondling his book, but then howled, "Can it be true? Don't be hasty, Asterius! Not after you've waited this long!" Muttering to himself then, he leaned over the book so far that his right eye socket was actually on it.

Witnessing this display, Dex slowly lost his nerve. He could plainly see Rash wasn't going to toss the book on his desk and walk away. However emboldened he felt, confronting the old man didn't seem like a wise idea. But all was not lost. There was this ledger, which sounded like a decent consolation prize.

The moment Dex set foot on the ground behind the warehouse, a voice hissed his name. "*Dexter! What on earth do you think you're doing?!*" It was Daphna. She'd nearly made his heart stop.

"I thought I'd see if I could swipe the book back for Dad," Dex said. "But the guy's like halfway making out with it."

"How could you go back in there after what he did to me?" Daphna demanded. "After what we've already figured out? How could you risk it? Are you an idiot?!" Daphna didn't mean to say that, and she could plainly see she'd lost Dex now. With a stony glare, he simply walked around her and onto the steps.

"Dex!" Daphna grabbed his arm. "I'm sorry, but you're being totally reckless!"

Dex snorted.

"I'm just scared, okay?" Daphna shouted. "I came back because I think I mixed up those two words and knew you'd remember. I saw you go back here, and I've been scared half-to-death."

"That's your problem," said Dex through

gritted teeth. "Now back off," he added, pulling his arm free. "I'm going to see if the ledger is up front before that pasty faced ape comes back."

"Dexter!" Daphna called as her brother bounded up the steps. "If you go in there, I'll—I'll call Latty, I swear." But Dex didn't even look back at her.

He was going to get himself killed.

flirting with disaster

Dex took a quick peek around the corner. No one was out front, so he edged along slowly until he could see into the store. The coast was clear. His sister was still pleading with him from the steps, but he no longer heard her. Opportunity was knocking way too loudly.

With a dash, he was inside.

That has to be the ledger, Dex thought. Right there on the desk was a large, crusty, official looking old book. A small fleet of regular sized books surrounded it, each lying open as well. This was going to be a breeze. He walked around behind the desk and scooped the book up, feeling like a master thief. But the book was far heavier even than it looked. It fell through his hands, hit the edge of the chair and landed under the desk. Dex got to his knees, amused: that might have been the first time he ever *un*intentionally dropped an old book.

Dexter got hold of the ledger and dragged it out, but just before he moved to stand, he heard the door open. "Wait, Emmet!" he heard Daphna shout.

Panicked, he slipped the ledger back on the desk and crouched underneath. "Come on," his sister was coaxing. She and Emmet had evidently stepped into the store. "I've been dying to talk to you since the first day I came in here," she said.

Emmet responded with stuttering. "Ah, um, I'm—I got to get back to work or the old man'll—"

"We could just get a slice of pizza," Daphna suggested. "On me."

There was a long pause. Dex sweated.

"I just think you're kind of cute is all."

Another painful pause.

Finally, Daphna said, "*Please, Emmet?*"

in a voice Dex had never heard. It was timid, but somehow not timid at all. It made him distinctly uncomfortable.

"I'll wait for you outside," Daphna said. The door opened and closed. She'd gone.

There was silence in the room, silence but for Emmet's increasingly stressed breathing. It seemed to stretch endlessly, but then, to Dex's profound relief, he heard the door open and close again.

After a few moments, Dex stood up and grabbed the ledger. But no sooner was it in his hands again than he heard the sound of shuffling feet from the other side of the closest stack of shelves. He froze. Two bony legs inside a brown robe were visible through a row of crooked books. Still clutching the ledger, Dex climbed back under the desk.

"I really love old books," Daphna said, *again*. "They're so—unique—and—different—" She was flailing. That had to be the eighth time she'd said the same thing in one way or another, but what else was there to say? Emmet hadn't uttered so much as a word the whole way to the pizza parlor, and he wouldn't look at her either. This was preferable, of course, even with the sunglasses, but still disconcerting.

Now they were sitting in a booth, and he was staring at his lap. Daphna was sure Dexter was safely out of the store by now, but she didn't know how to get away. If her brother was okay, the first thing she was going to do when she saw him was kill him.

Finally, Emmet spoke, though without looking up. "I never thought another girl would be nice to me," he said. Then he blurted, "Once there were lots of girls—and lots of boys—and they were all nice to me. He says it's a dream." Emmet didn't continue. He seemed to drift into thought.

It was obvious that this boy was seriously disturbed, but she'd gotten this far, and so easily. Daphna never thought she was capable of flirting, but it worked just the way it did for the Pop girls who made eyes at boys in school when they wanted favors. It just came to her in desperation. All she did was say 'please' in that corny shy voice while batting her eyes a few times. And it worked like a charm! Emmet seemed almost harmless now.

Maybe, since she was here with him, she could be more than just a distraction. Maybe she could get some real information. "Emmet," Daphna whispered, "What's going on? What does Rash want?"

"Words of course," Emmet said, but nothing more.

"That book my dad gave Rash," Daphna pressed, "do you know what it is?"

"Could be some book he's been looking for," Emmet answered, flatly. "A book he thought was destroyed. He's not sure yet, though. Kept me up all night trying to read it to him, but I—can't anymore." Then he added sharply, "That's all I'm sayin'."

Daphna reached out and put her hand

on Emmet's. He looked up, not at her, but at her hand.

"Emmet," she said softly, "is Rash going to fire you?"

This did the trick. Emmet flashed her a quick look, then forced his eyes back down. "*What do you mean?*" he demanded. "What did he tell you?"

"He asked me if I wanted to be his new assistant," Daphna said.

If it were possible, Emmet paled. His jaw clenched.

"But I'm not going to do it," Daphna hastened to add, sensing she'd hit a bull's-eye. "I told him no—here, I'll make you a deal," she said. "If you tell me what you know, I'll tell you what I know."

"What did he say!"

"You first," Daphna insisted. Then, before he could object, she asked, "Is my father involved with Rash?"

"You are," Emmet said, startling her. But he startled Daphna even more by adding,

"You and your mother."

"My *mother?*"

"He doesn't tell me anything," Emmet explained, "but once, when I was a kid, I was reading him the newspaper. He was blind back then, too. That's why he saved me, to help him. I know I'm not the first, 'cause sometimes he calls me other names. He's bull-headed, but he's a good man to put up with me. He's gonna let me do it soon."

"Yes," Daphna said, hoping she sounded encouraging rather than chilled. She gave Emmet's hand a slight squeeze, which got him talking again.

"I read him this article about how a book lady got killed in some caves somewhere in Turkey," Emmet said. "Rash laughed like crazy, but when I read she was a mother, he went berserk and started screaming, 'She already found it! She already found it!' And then he actually started crying."

"Crying?"

"I asked him why, and he said because if

she got married and had a kid, then she must have found it and destroyed it—some really special book I guess they were both looking for. But then, when he calmed down, he said all was not lost, and that we'd need her kid. We were going to move to Israel where she lived, but he found out you moved to Portland, so we came here right away."

"But that was thirteen years ago," Daphna gasped. "You've been here all that time?"

Emmet nodded. "In the warehouse. Only we weren't open for business. We've been working and waiting."

"For what? Wait, Emmet, are you saying you've been in the warehouse for *thirteen years* reading books for Rash? And you never came out?"

"Only sometimes, at night," Emmet admitted. "I go to your house to make sure you haven't moved. But this year he's been letting me hunt. He's been promising for so long."

An icy revulsion passed over Daphna

at the thought of Emmet spying on her. And she didn't want to ask what this hunting was about.

"What," she asked, "what were you waiting for?"

"For you to turn thirteen," Emmet said.

"Why? What's all this about thirteen?"

"Don't know. We were going to grab you today, but that was before your father gave him that book, if it is that book, if your mother didn't destroy it. I guess it is if he let you go. Now you tell me," Emmet demanded.

Daphna had nearly forgotten her offer. Her mind was reeling from this overload of information. Her mother had been looking for this book, too?

"Rash hypnotizes people," she managed. "He uses some kind of mesmerizing words, but you don't remember unless someone tells you what really happened."

This information seemed to sink in slowly with Emmet, who sat impassively after hearing it. But then he said to his knees,

"He doesn't do it to me. I know what he does to other people. He knows special words. We collect them. But he doesn't do it to me. He even tried to teach me when I turned thirteen, but I couldn't do it. I'm too stupid. He's been good to me." Emmet hesitated, then flashed that sickening smile. "And now that he's got his book," he declared, "I know he'll let me do it! I thought it was going to be you. Maybe it will be anyway."

"What is it you want to do so badly?"

"Kill someone."

Daphna, who'd kept her hand on Emmet's through all of this, snatched it back like she'd been burned, but she managed to pretend she needed to cover a cough. Then she said she needed to use the restroom and excused herself. After slipping out the back door of the parlor, she ran for her life.

The sandals shuffled slowly but inexorably toward the entry room. Why he didn't bolt immediately was beyond Dex. He peeked over the desk, hoping to judge that the distance to the door was short enough for a sprint, but he was met with a shock.

Ruby! Standing right there! She'd apparently come out of a hall on the other end of the room and was now looking him straight in the eye. Dex, paralyzed, simply stared at her vivid white hair and elaborately wrinkled face, unable to dip back out of sight.

But then, to his amazement, she put a finger to her lips and motioned for him to get down. Dex ducked under the desk one more time, just as Rash appeared in the entry room.

"Patience, patience now, old man," Rash counseled himself. He approached the desk and began feeling around on top.

"Emmet!" he hollered after finding it bare. "*Where is my list?!*" When no answer came, he pounded his cracked cane inches above Dex's head.

"Excuse me, Sir!" said a woman's voice—Ruby's. Dex had somehow forgotten she was there.

The sandal stopped and turned. "May I help you?" Rash snapped.

"Yes, thank you ever so much. Could I trouble you for just a moment? I seem to be unable to find the section on Argentine knife-fighting charms. Do you think you could lead me there? Oh, dear. You can't see! I'm dreadfully sorry."

"Who are you?" Rash demanded. "I know your voice."

"How strange," said Ruby. "I do come in here a lot. Is this a bad time?"

"Of course not," Rash replied. "I know this place perfectly. If you would be so kind as to follow me. I am expecting my useless assistant to return at any moment. I have urgent business."

"Oh, I understand completely. Good help is so hard to find these days. I'm sorry to bother."

And with that, the robe shuffled away, and the two elderly people disappeared into the store.

There was no hesitating this time. Dex broke for the front door. He half expected to run into Daphna and Emmet out front, but they weren't there, so he dashed across the street and slipped back into the alley.

He'd done it!

But the elation was short lived. By the time Dex's nerves had settled, he felt only a powerful wave of a very familiar feeling. Did he really think he was going to be able to use this book? Who was he kidding? Ruby would probably think he was crazy, a crazy thief. And now that he'd told Daphna what he was doing, she would want to see it, especially since she'd helped him. In fact, she'd probably only helped when she realized what they might get. Yes, she would demand to see the ledger, and this struck Dexter as the worst possible result of all his efforts.

The noise of a large vehicle attracted Dex's attention. A garbage truck pulled to a stop at the curb directly in front of the alley. As soon as he saw it, Dex's instincts took over. He approached the truck, and without looking even one more time at the large book in his hands, he tossed it into the scoop. Dex watched it get dumped into the midst of tons of garbage. The sight of it buoyed his flagging spirits.

Then he saw Daphna. She was padding nervously toward the store, trying to peek in unnoticed. Dex sighed. He poked his head out of the alley and whistled. At first, Daphna looked relieved, then furious. She stormed across the street.

"Dexter!" Daphna roared, "How could you be so irresponsible! Anything could have happened to you in there! And I had to lure Emmet away for you! He's a maniac! He's wants to kill someone, Dexter, actually *kill* someone! What if he'd hurt me! What if Rash had gotten hold of you! What if—" but Daphna was running out of steam because what she'd learned from Emmet was suddenly overwhelming her anger.

"Dex," she said, calm but panting,

"Dad's not involved in all this—*Mom is*."

Dex had been waiting for his sister to stop ranting so he could tell her off again, but he was taken completely off guard by this news. Daphna shared the gist of what she'd gotten out of Emmet.

"So, hold on," Dex said when she finished. "He figured if Mom had gotten married and had kids, then she must've found some book and gotten rid of it? What's one thing got to do with the other? Was she searching for it every minute of her life or something?"

"Maybe," Daphna said. "Maybe I was right and it is full of hypnotic words. Maybe Mom thought it was evil or something. But Rash has a lot of words. Emmet told me they collect them. I think that's what the ledger is, Dex. You said Rash needed to find something in it to verify the book Dad gave him, right? Did you get it? Did you hide it or something?"

"Got rid of it," Dex said. "A certain old and cruddy book is off to the city dump."

For a moment, Daphna wasn't sure how to react. If Rash needed that ledger, she was glad they'd taken it—but why throw it away so quickly? Now that their Mom was part of all this, she felt a burning desire to get to the bottom of it. "Did you at least look at it?" she asked.

"It was just a bunch of chicken scratch," Dex lied. "Totally illegible."

"But Dexter," Daphna protested, "I'm good at deciphering sloppy work. Now we have no way of knowing what it was."

"Sue me then!" Dex snarled. Of course he'd done the wrong thing. He always did the wrong thing. His mother was involved? It didn't matter. He'd had enough. "I don't see what you're worried about," Dex added. "I'm sure if you flirt with that Neanderthal some more, he'll tell you everything you want to know."

"*What?!* I did that for you! I probably risked my life!"

"Did I ask you to?" Dex retorted. But he

knew, he always knew, when he was being a jerk. It just didn't matter. Dex had an incredible urge to shove his sister, but instead he walked away.

Daphna was livid. She didn't understand why her brother was such a certifiable lunatic sometimes, and right out of the blue. He could be perfectly normal, even halfway nice one minute, then go mental the next. Throwing away that ledger was exactly the kind of thoughtless thing he'd do.

Daphna stood there shaking her head. But then she remembered her father.

entries and exits

Dex headed home. He was finished with all this nonsense. Of course he arrived at the same time Daphna did. Brother and sister glared at each other as they headed in the back door. They were both pleased, though, to see sandwiches sitting on the kitchen table. Less pleasing was Latty's half-crazed expression.

"Look," Daphna said, trying to head off an agonized plea, "we're sorry, really, but all kinds of crazy things are going on." The moment she said this, Daphna realized Latty might very well be able to shed some light on the craziness.

"Was Mom searching for one really special book," she asked, "a book she wanted to get rid of? Maybe kind of, well, a hypnotism book? You said you heard of Mr. Rash, right? Is there any chance he was looking for it, too?"

Latty looked stricken. "Did—did you go see that vile man this morning? I told you," she sputtered, coming unhinged in a way neither twin had previously witnessed. "I insisted!"

"But Dad—"

"This is positively the last straw!" Latty wailed. "You—you are both—grounded! You are not to leave this house until—until school starts! And if I have to stay home and watch you every second, I will! Do you hear me?! What can I say to make you two understand how worried I get?!"

"But Dad called—!" Daphna again attempted to protest.

"I don't want to hear it!" Latty railed.

"You can't ground us!" Dex roared. *"YOU'RE NOT OUR MOTHER!"*

These were words neither twin had ever uttered before. Daphna was shocked to hear them, but not sorry.

Latty looked mortally wounded. She didn't seem to know what to say, but it didn't matter because just then, in through the back door wobbled a very unsteady Milton Wax. He looked awful. His face was gaunt, and his eyes rolled vacantly. Dex and Daphna looked at each other and immediately forgot about Latty.

"You're ill!" Latty cried, rushing to Milton's aid. In a flash, she had him sitting at the table with a cold compress on his forehead.

"No, no," Milton muttered to no one in particular. "Winded is all. Long morning. I've been doing some thinking."

For a moment, and despite all that had happened, both Dex and Daphna thought there was still a chance he'd been out finding gifts. But he hadn't come in with anything, and he sat down without acknowledging their presence.

"I don't know what's gotten into me," he

finally admitted. "Went by that shop again. I think there might have been some misunderstanding about the book I brought in yesterday."

"Yes!" Daphna encouraged. "He—he tricked you into giving it to him—"

"Mr. Rash was in a terrible state," Milton said, giving Daphna a puzzled look. "He was waving that broken cane around like a madman."

"What's going on?" the twins asked, breathless.

"Lost," Milton said, but he was looking off somewhere between or above the twins. "Some valuable book was lost. Irreplaceable, apparently. He had that big boy searching high and low."

Dex and Daphna exchanged worried but pleased glances.

Milton went on, "Mr. Rash did calm down a bit. He asked me to find a certain book for him, something he'd owned in the past. I told him I had an idea of someone who might have a copy—old Berny Quartich, actually."

"You didn't tell him who had it, did you?" Daphna asked.

"Of course not," Milton replied.

"Dad, about yesterday," said Daphna, "when you met with Mr. Rash—"

"Mr. Rash said he'd consider renegotiating the sale of my book if I could get it for him quickly," Milton said. "I'll just head on over—"

"You'll do no such thing, Mr. Milton Adam Wax!" Latty declared. "You will go straight up to bed and stay there until you get some life back in you."

"Dad!" Daphna tried again. "He hypnotized you! He knows words that can—"

"Daphna!" Latty scolded. "Don't be absurd!" She was ushering Milton out of the kitchen.

Like an ailing child, he wasn't resisting at all, and he'd shown no discernable reaction to Daphna's revelation.

A wave of distaste washed over Dex as he watched.

Daphna realized her father was getting very, very old. *So weak* was the thought that crossed both their minds.

"Dad!" Dexter called out before he was whisked away entirely. "What's the book called? The one Rash wants you to get?"

Again, Milton looked confused. "A Latin book," he managed.

"What's it called?" the twins asked.

"Did I mention it was Latin? Perhaps I'll track it down tomorrow."

"*But what is it called?*"

"*Videre Per Alterum.*"

"What does that mean?"

Instead of replying, Milton paled further and went weak in the knees. He clutched at Latty.

"That does it!" she cried. "Can't you two hooligans see your father isn't well? We're going to the hospital, Milton." She reversed course and herded him to the door.

"Wait!" Daphna called before they'd gone. "Galice!"

Dex shook his head. "Kalice!" he shouted. Then, "Graal!"

Milton offered no reaction.

Latty did though. "What is wrong with you, two?" she demanded, clearly disgusted. "Is this a time for nonsense?! And don't you dare leave this house. Do you hear me! We'll be right back!" And with that, she hauled Milton out to the car and drove off.

When they were gone, Daphna turned to Dex. "What are we going to do now?" she asked. "Telling Dad didn't make him remember. I'm sure it's because he saw Rash again today!"

"Did you hear how mad Rash is?" Dex said. He couldn't prevent a smirk.

"Yeah," Daphna replied. She allowed a smile too, but only momentarily. "Dex, we've got to help Dad, but we don't know what Rash did to him." She thought a moment longer, then said, "We might have been able to find something in that ledger to help, but that's out, so we've got to find out what this new book is, this Latin book. They must be connected."

"Daphna, I'm sorry I threw the ledger away," Dex said. "As usual, I was wrong, okay?"

"Dex, I wasn't—"

"Anyway, Dad won't be going anywhere for a while. When they get back, Latty will probably barricade his room. She'll guard the door for a week if she has to."

"That would be lucky," Daphna said. "But she'd probably lock us in there with him. I hope she's just being paranoid, though. She's totally snapped! She grounded us, Dex! I'm sorry, but there's no way—you don't think it's serious, do you? Dad, I mean."

"No," Dex said with reasonable confidence. "You know how Latty gets when we're sick. And she can't ground us. We don't get grounded."

"Yeah," said Daphna, comforted. "We'll

talk her down later. Maybe since she knew Rash, she's been thinking about Mom. You know she gets extra protective every time that happens."

"Whatever," Dex replied. "She needs to get over it. It's been *thirteen years.*"

"Hey," said Daphna, "what if Dad isn't the only one Rash has looking for this Latin book?"

"That just means we better get a move on it." Somehow Dex was still involved in all this. He had to admit now that he wanted to be.

Daphna was glad not to be in this alone, even if her brother's "help" meant more hassles.

"Hey!" she said again, "maybe we can find a copy on the web and order it! There are tons of rare book sites. Come on." Daphna headed into the office. It only took a few seconds to call up one of the bookmarked sites. "What was it called again, that Latin book?"

"*Videre Per Alterum.*"

"Can you type that in for me?"

"What am I, your slave?" Dex snapped. "Are you crippled or something?"

"No, Dexter! I just have no idea how to spell it."

"And I know Latin?"

"Fine. Whatever," Daphna shot back, just barely resisting the urge to make a crack about Dex not knowing French either. Here it was again, Mr. Schitzo acting like a normal person one minute and a crazy one the next.

She did the best she could trying to type in the title, but her search came up with nothing.

"Wait!" Daphna cried when the disappointment passed. "Dad's got an old Latin dictionary. I was just looking up some stuff last week!"

Dex rolled his eyes as Daphna scampered to the living room. She returned a few moments later waving a tall, skinny, old-looking book.

"Got it!" she said. "A ha!"

"What?"

"This is where I'd seen a book shaped like this," Daphna said. "That book Dad gave Rash. It was in this same funny shape. Long and narrow. Except of course it was mangled half-to-death."

"*And?*"

"It's been bugging me is all." Daphna opened the dictionary and paged through.

Dex watched his sister, feeling as though he ought to be helping in some way. He couldn't think of anything to do, so he said, "That looks like a pretty old book."

"Oh, it is," Daphna agreed in that annoying, I'm-an-expert voice. "It's very rare, worth eight or nine hundred bucks, I bet. We've got to be careful or it'll get damaged."

"Who cares!" Dex couldn't feign interest any longer. "Find the words already, would you? Videre—Per—Alterum."

Daphna blinked. "Fine. Jeez! You're the one who asked." She flipped to the back pages. "Oh, there's a list of prefixes back here," she said. "Here's 'per,' right here. It means, 'through.' Okay, so let's find 'Videre,' since I'm near the back anyway. Hmmm—"

Dexter huffed impatiently as Daphna flipped back a few pages with her tongue sticking out of the side of her mouth.

"Videre," she read, her eyes having zeroed in on their target. "It means, 'To see.' Right then. So far, we've got, 'To see through." She was already turning to the front of the book, and she had the last word in just a few seconds. "Others!" she declared. "'Alterum' means, 'others'—*To see through others.*"

"What does that mean?" Dex asked. "What's that got to do with hypnotism?" Then, jesting, he added, "Maybe he wants x-ray vision, too."

This didn't sound as farfetched as it might have, the twins both realized, but it didn't seem right.

Daphna thought a moment. "Well," she said, "it says 'see through others' not 'see through things.' 'Others' sounds like people, doesn't it? I've got it! He wants to read people's minds! He wants to be psychic! Dex, I can't believe all this stuff might actually be real."

The twins paused to consider this new theory. It was certainly a much better guess. But after a moment, Dex said, "I don't think that's right. I mean, how would that help him know if the book Dad already gave him is the one he's looking for?"

"I don't know," Daphna replied. "Actually, it kind of seems like he can read people's minds now. I mean, when Dad and I went in there, he demanded the book right away, like he already had an idea what it was. By the way, I forgot to tell you—Emmet told me they've known about us for our whole lives. He's been watching our house at night. That *really* freaks me out."

It freaked Dexter out too, but he preferred not to think about it just then. "How did Rash know something was going on in the back of the store, when I was on the loft?" he asked. "With Emmet and—Wait a minute!" Dex cried. "It has something to do with Emmet! Emmet was there when you and Dad came in right? Emmet was in the back when I was on the loft, and—he knows when Emmet is out hunting or whatever."

"Are we saying Rash reads Emmet's mind?" Daphna asked.

"I don't know," Dex said, thinking back over what they'd seen between Emmet and Rash. Mind reading didn't quite make sense.

"No," Dex concluded after further consideration. "Emmet would never have gone off with you and told you all that stuff if Rash could read his mind. Didn't you say he wouldn't look at you? I wonder—"

"*That's it!*" Daphna whooped. The truth had dawned on her at once. "He *can* see. To see through others! Rash can see through Emmet's eyes! That's why he wouldn't look at me—so Rash wouldn't know I was with him!

"Emmet saw Dad and me come in, and

then Rash saw the book when Emmet looked at it. And that's why he started banging his cane on the table!"

"And that's why he knew what we looked like."

It felt good to find the pieces falling together, even if it was also frightening.

"But now Emmet is going blind, too," Dexter said. Then he got it. "He needs the word that will let him do that again, with you, from that book dad's getting him!"

"Right! So it makes sense that Rash wants to make me his new assistant! You know, I think he was going to try to teach me to use those words—in the ledger—before he got that book of nonsense. I'll bet he was going to force me to do something for him. But now he wants me to look for this—"

"First Tongue thing."

"Right! What is that? Wait a sec." Daphna turned and typed the phrase into a search engine she called up. Nothing looked useful.

"Hold on," she said, returning to the rare book site. She copied in *Videre Per Alterum*, spelled correctly, but to no avail. It didn't come up in any of the other book related sites either. Conceding, Daphna moaned, "I don't know what to do, Dex. We need to stop Dad from getting that book. Maybe we should just tell him all this when he gets back."

"It won't matter," Dex said. "Rash got to him again, remember?"

"Then, I guess I could go with him when he gets it and, I don't know, grab it? When do you think they'll be back? I think we ought to keep looking for info on this First Tongue. Maybe if we figure out what Rash is really after, we can do something about it. We need some answers, Dex, fast."

Dex couldn't agree more. "I think I'll walk up to the library and see what they have," he said.

Daphna looked amazed, but he ignored her.

"They've got tons of stuff on myths

and legends, right?" said Dex. "They probably have books with magic spells and all that kind of stuff. You can wait here in case Dad gets back and tries to go for the Latin book—*What?*"

"Nothing," Daphna said. "I mean that's great. I—I was just thinking maybe you might want to wait here. I mean, since I know exactly where all those books are at the—"

"You're welcome to come with me," Dex said, trying to control his tone. Of course Daphna wanted to be the one to figure it all out. "But I'm not staying here."

Daphna looked miffed, but managed to stifle whatever she wanted to say. "Fine," is what came out. "Check out anything you can find and bring it right home, okay?"

"Right," Dex said, knowing he'd do nothing of the sort.

surprise! (part one)

He heard the crying the moment he stepped back inside. Dex had reached the end of the driveway when he realized he'd forgotten his sweatshirt, and so turned back. It was Daphna, in her room. Dex tiptoed near and found her door ajar.

Sniffling now, Daphna was dialing the phone. "Hello?" she said, hesitantly, "Is this Wren's mom? Um—um—this is—this is—I'm sorry, is—I was just wondering—is—Wren home—from camp yet?"

There was a pause.

"Summer camp?" Daphna clarified, though weakly. "In California?"

Another pause.

"I see," Daphna croaked. "No, I must have made a mistake. No message. I'm sure

I'll see her around. Thank you." She waited, then slammed the receiver down. Then,
nothing.

They really aren't at camp! Dexter
thought. And he'd made that up! Oh, this was
rich. Dex actually had to cover his mouth,
but then he heard crying again. It was different this time. Daphna was sobbing violently.
It sounded like actual, physical pain. The
thought crossed Dex's mind that he ought to
comfort his sister. He even took a step toward
the door, but what could he possibly say? Not
a single word came to mind.

Instead, Dex stole away. He was the last
person Daphna would want to talk to right
now. He grabbed his sweatshirt from the
floor in the laundry room, threw it on, then
headed back outside and on his way.

Dex broke into a jog. It was time to see
Ruby. He hadn't been sure he wanted to see
her today, despite her request for a birthday
visit. But not any more. He needed to know
why she'd helped him with Rash.

Dex picked up the pace, heading straight for the Multnomah Village Rest and Rehabilitation Home.

Daphna cried so hard, she actually threw up. Sullenly, she balled up her blanket and sheets for the wash. Wren and Teal weren't even on her mind while she and Dex were trying to figure out what was going on. But the second her brother left the house, she was blindsided by the need to find out whether she'd been lied to or not.

The truth was devastating. She was no better off than Dexter! Maybe she was worse off. At least he didn't delude himself. *They lied!* Wren and Teal, smiling right to her face on the last day of school! And all she wanted to do was hang out once in a while, maybe get some pointers about the cool way they wore their hair. She'd even dared to hope they might let her show them the ABC. After all the help she'd given them with, with everything!

Daphna wanted to go on a rampage. She wanted to break things. Big things. She wanted to destroy her room, the entire house and everything in it, books and all. No, not the books—

The R & R!

Daphna had a reading session scheduled at the Home—in half an hour! It had completely slipped her mind.

Great, she thought. Maybe she should just skip it. Yes, she should skip it. There was way too much going on. The last thing Daphna wanted to do now was read to a bunch of silly old people, half of whom drifted off or didn't pay attention to her anyway. *But*, she thought, *they'd sit there waiting for her all afternoon*. Daphna couldn't do that to them. *I'll tell them I'm not feeling well.* She grabbed the phone and called, but the line was busy. She tried again, but had no luck. When she put the phone down, it rang.

It was Latty. "Oh, thank goodness!" she sighed. "Is everything okay?"

"How's Dad?" Daphna asked.

"He's okay. Resting. They think its just exhaustion. We'll be home in a couple of hours. I just wanted to make sure everything's okay."

Daphna was relieved. "Latty," she said, "about Mom, and Mr. Rash—"

"Daphna," Latty interrupted, "I don't know anything about a book they were both looking for. But I told you, under no circumstances should you have anything to do with that vile man. And you're not to leave the house. Let me speak to Dexter."

"He left."

"*What?*"

"And I'm leaving, too," Daphna said, though she didn't mean it. Then she hung up without saying good-bye. That felt really good.

Of course the phone rang immediately, but Daphna wasn't picking up. And since she was obviously facing several hours cooped up listening to it ring, she decided she would leave. She'd run over to the R & R to say she was sick in person, then head to the library to do some proper research. Even if Dex had finally decided to show some initiative, she couldn't imagine he had the slightest idea what to do. As soon as this was decided, Daphna hurried off. The phone was still ringing.

Even though his sister was at home, Dex took a few unnecessary side streets along his way to the familiar, odd building. But here it was with its slightly bowed walls. It was an old wooden thing, and together with the funny little structure on the roof, the place reminded him of all those pictures of Noah's Ark he'd colored so incompetently as a child.

Dex pulled his hood down over his face, then slipped inside through the service entrance. No one ever saw him come in, but he wasn't taking chances. The employee elevator took him to the third floor, and when he saw the hall was empty, he ran to room 306 and knocked quickly. There was no answer, so he knocked again. He hadn't considered the possibility Ruby wouldn't be home.

As he waited, a door at the end of the hall opened and an old woman leaned out. Dex looked over at her, but then back at the door quickly. He knocked impatiently. The old lady was coming down the hall. It was stupid he knew, but Dex did not like being seen there—by anyone. He was just about to turn and run, but the door finally opened. He dashed inside.

Fifteen minutes later, Daphna walked through the front doors of The R & R, three floors below.

"Ah, Daphna!" cooed the Home's director from her orderly desk in the lobby. Her name was Evelyn Idun. "I was worried you weren't going to make it today. You're always so early," she said, pushing her pointy glasses up her pointy nose.

Everything about Evelyn was pointy.

She was tall and strikingly skinny, and her shoulders, knees and elbows seemed to point this way and that like one of those signposts that shows the way to several cities at once. At the same time, her skin looked slightly baggy. It wasn't that she looked really old—Daphna figured she was in her sixties. It looked more like she'd lost a lot of weight too quickly.

"But of course," Evelyn added with a smile, "you never miss an appointment."

"Oh, well, I'm—I'm feeling kinda lousy actually," Daphna muttered. It wasn't a complete lie. She felt about as badly as she ever had in her life.

"Oh, no!" Evelyn said, her face creasing with concern. "I hope it's nothing serious. You should, but—"

Daphna hoped she was going to tell her to head back home. That way, she'd only be going along with the suggestion.

"Well," Evelyn said, "I think maybe you should just run on up to the lounge and say hello. Tell everyone you're not feeling well. They'll understand if you can't stay."

Daphna considered asking Evelyn to make apologies for her, but she felt too guilty. "Okay," she sighed. "You're right. The Dwarves will understand."

"What's that, Daphna, doll?"

"Oh, nothing. I'm sorry. I'll just head on up now."

"Grand. You are an angel, Daphna Wax!"

Daphna grinned, despite herself.

"Oh," Evelyn added, her eyes narrowing playfully, "tell that father of yours he ought to return his friends' calls once in a while." She always said that, and Daphna always did, even though she'd given up a long time ago on the possibility of her father ever dating Eveyln.

Daphna rode the elevator up to the third floor, wondering at herself for calling her group the 'Dwarves' in front of Evelyn. She'd secretly dubbed her reading group 'The Seven Dwarves' because they were all short and kind of silly, and, of course, because there were seven of them. How embarrassing. She was really losing it.

When the elevator opened, Daphna walked slowly toward the lounge at the end of the hall, trying to look as awful as she felt. She almost wished Dex were around to give her some advice since he faked being sick at least once a month to make Latty keep him home from school. Daphna had never done that in her entire life. She took a deep breath and walked into the orange-carpeted lounge.

"*SURPRISE!*"

Seven feeble but festive voices greeted Daphna's entrance, and a rain of fairly pitiful but well-intentioned streamers wafted toward her feet. "*HAPPY BIRTHDAY!*" the group wheezed and then weakly tooted party horns.

Daphna looked around at all the old faces smiling at her. As usual, everyone talked at once in their various funny accents, wishing her happiness and health and long life and a good marriage with many children and a dozen other things she couldn't hear. When Daphna saw the collection of cafeteria cupcakes sitting on the card table in the center of the room, she was so touched that she momentarily forgot the troubles that seemed to have come out of nowhere in the last twenty-four hours. Just those two little words, 'Happy Birthday,' were a balm that soothed her aching mind.

There was Mrs. Kunyan, beaming with her red cheeks and mile-wide smile. And there was Mrs. Deucalion in her floral housedress and fuzzy slippers nudging bashful Mr. Dwyfan to show more enthusiasm. Mr. Tumbainot was in fine health today, but he often seemed to have a cold when Daphna read to the group and interrupted her with his thunderous sneezing. Mr. Hina winked his lazy eye at her. It made him look sleepy all the time, but of course they all looked sleepy all the time to Daphna. Even grumpy Mr. Bergelmir was grinning. Mrs. Tapi was too, although as usual she was distracted by the little silver pill box she was always sorting through. Yes, the Dwarves were all there, and Daphna was glad.

"A teenager!" Mrs. Deucalion cooed. "How does it feel? I can't remember, myself. Too long ago! Much too long ago!"

Here goes nothing, Daphna thought. "Actually, I'm not feeling very well. Thank you all so much, though."

"Not feeling well?!" cried Mr. Hina. Every face in the room went serious. The entire group rushed to her—or rushed, Daphna thought, in the way an anxious ring of ancient sea turtles might rush.

"Nothing serious, I hope," said Mrs. Kunyan, the first to reach Daphna. "We were so looking forward to your visit today." The others were simultaneously expressing their concerns and offering advice on what remedies she ought to seek right away.

"No, no, I'm okay. I just—" Daphna groped for words. The excessive concern everyone was showing made her feel terribly uncomfortable. They were acting like it was some sort of medical emergency. Didn't they have anything more to look forward to than hearing her read? Daphna didn't want to get old if it meant ending up so needy like these people, however nice they were.

"You're sweating!" Mrs. Tapi fretted. "You should go home and rest."

"Yes," Daphna said quietly, looking down at the carpet. She *was* sweating.

"Maybe you'll come back after dinner?" This was Mr. Tumbainot. His unified ivory brow lifted expectantly. Everyone fell silent, waiting for Daphna's reply with an embarrassing amount of expectation. It was ridiculous!

Daphna meant to say no—how could she possibly say yes with all the chaos raging around her? But when she looked around at all the kindly, eager faces, she wavered. Then she caved. Saying no would be like telling a classroom full of kids they couldn't have the candy they were promised. "Sure," she said, "I'll do my best."

"Wonderful!" announced Mr. Bergelmir, clapping his hands. Everyone concurred that this was wonderful. He put a hand on Daphna's shoulder and walked her into the hall. "We will look forward to your return, Daphna," he said, then turned and closed the door on a vigorous conversation in the lounge.

surprise! (part two)

Halfway down the hall, in front of room 306, Daphna stopped to check her watch. At the same moment, she heard a voice from behind the door.

"I hate them all!" it shouted.

Daphna knew that voice. But it couldn't be. She pressed her ear against the door.

"As I have so often told you," a woman was saying, "this world is a pitiless place. The uncommon find few friends. Even those closest to you sometimes cannot be trusted. Find an ally who can help you put your anger in the right place."

A boy answered. "I wish I could live with you."

Unless Daphna was crazy, which wasn't out of the realm of possibility at this point, that was her brother's voice. But it couldn't be. It had to be someone's grandson with a voice—*exactly*—like Dex's.

Daphna pushed her ear harder into the door.

"Oh, my dear boy, if only that were—"

The door was suddenly opened by an old woman. Daphna must have rattled it. And she was with—Dex.

Unglued at the sight of his sister, Dexter leapt from a couch. The woman, who had exquisitely wrinkled skin and brilliant white hair, stood looking at Daphna, who was looking at Dexter, astonished.

"Daphna!" the woman said, breaking into a smile. But as far as Daphna knew, she'd never seen this person before.

"Dex, what are you doing here?" Daphna blurted, finding her voice at last.

Defeated, Dex slumped back onto the couch. He'd completely forgotten she was supposed to come today. "Perfect," he spat.

"Perfect indeed!" the woman declared.

She was heavyset, but spry, and she bowed formally. "Daphna Wax," she said, "my name is Ruby Scharlach. I have been looking forward to meeting you for a very long time. Your brother here, I have known for many months now."

"Wait a minute!" Daphna exclaimed. "I do know you! I've seen you in the ABC!"

"The bookshop? Indeed, though I doubt you've seen me as often as I've seen you there! You hardly notice a thing but the books!"

"I—I don't understand," Daphna said, turning to her brother, but he wouldn't meet her eye.

"Let me illuminate," said Ruby. "Have a seat, Daphna. Have some tea. There are extraordinary things to impart, and I sincerely hope you are ready to hear them."

There was nothing else to do. Daphna sat down next to her brother and poured herself a cup of tea from a kettle sitting on the coffee table.

Ruby waited for Daphna to finish pouring. "Today, your birthday," she said, "is the perfect day for us all to finally meet and talk! You both mean so very much to me."

"But—I don't understand," said Daphna.

"You will," Ruby assured. "The first thing you should know—and I was just about to share this with your brother—is that I am well aware that something dreadful is afoot at Asterius' bookshop. As you so keenly noted, Daphna, I've been keeping an eye on it for some time. The second thing you should know is that long before she took the name Shimona or Wax, I was a dear, dear friend of your mother's."

Dex bolted upright from the corpse-like position he'd assumed.

"What?" he cried. "You knew our mom? Why didn't you ever tell me?"

"That is part of what I was planning to tell you today, Dex. A conflict long at rest has been set in motion once again, and I need your help."

Daphna shook her head as if trying to wake herself from a dream.

"Wait a minute," she said. "How do you two know each other? I don't understand."

"I was Dexter's tutor last semester," was Ruby's simple reply. Daphna's mouth fell open, which caused Ruby to turn toward Dex. "I'm sorry to expose our little secret," she said softly, "but I trust you will soon see this as an insignificant betrayal."

Humiliated, Dex looked down.

"I wanted to get to know you twins," Ruby explained. "When I moved to town, the first thing I did was call. Dex here picked up the phone and—I'm sorry not to have told you of my little deception before Dexy—I offered my tutorial services to both of you. He told me you could probably tutor me, but he agreed to come. I was going to think of another sneaky way to get to know you, Daphna dear, this year. The truth is, though, I don't think you need any preparation to hear what I have to say." Daphna couldn't help but feel pleased to be told she was already prepared for—whatever it was.

Dex was anything but pleased, but at least now he understood why not much tutoring ever actually happened during his tutoring sessions. He and Ruby usually just talked about life, which was fine by him. She listened to everything he had to say. She believed him when he said his father didn't care about him. She believed him when he told her he couldn't hang out with anyone at school. The way Ruby knit her amazingly wrinkled brow and nodded at his complaints was worth a dozen 'F's. She was the only person in the world he'd told about the Clearing.

"So what's going on?" Daphna asked, trying now not to look at Dexter, whose expression looked like an open wound.

"I wish I could tell you exactly what Asterius is planning," Ruby said, "but there is much I can share that might help."

"We figured some of it out," Daphna said.

Ruby looked intrigued. "Please," she invited.

"It's all about a book," Daphna explained. "Rash is after some kind of book, maybe one full of, I guess, magical words. He's already got one book with a list of words that hypnotize people, a ledger—or, he had one. Dex stole it and threw it out. He—I guess he was coming here to kidnap me, to make me learn them or something, I guess 'cause his assistant is going blind, I'm not sure, but then my father might have given him this book he's really after, a book Mom was after, too."

"He read some news story about Mom getting killed and figured she'd found it and destroyed it," Dex put in, suddenly thinking well of his trashing the ledger. Ruby hadn't shown any reaction more than a raised brow upon learning its fate.

"For some reason," Dex continued, "Rash figured if Mom had gotten married and had a kid, she must have done that."

"But Rash still wants me to go away with him, after he remembers how to see through my eyes. He wants me to study this book, if it is the book, and look for something called the First Tongue, but we have no idea what that is. I just don't see why he wants me for all this."

Ruby looked impressed. The twins found this reassuring, but hearing themselves tell their story made them both suspect they'd gone round the bend.

"I don't think he came for you specifically, dear," Ruby said to Daphna. "I'm sure either of you would have sufficed. It's just that you got delivered, it seems, along with that book. Tell me about it, would you?"

"Well," Daphna said, her tone faltering slightly.

Dexter smirked. He'd seen it—it was only for a second—but Daphna definitely looked crestfallen to hear Rash wasn't especially after her. Dex wanted to ridicule her for all he was worth, but now was obviously not the time.

"I do know my Dad found it in Turkey," Daphna was saying. "Wait a sec! That's where Mom got killed! Why didn't I think of that before!"

"The book is full of nonsense," Dexter said, wondering if this coincidence meant something.

"Rash made me read the same line in it, like a million times," said Daphna. "Do you know what it is? Do you know what the First Tongue is? There was nothing on the Web. I haven't had a chance to check the library—"

"You'd find nothing," Ruby said. "But you've come to the right place."

"Tell us!" the twins begged.

"The First Tongue is a language, quite possibly the first," Ruby explained. "Regardless, what's important is that it possesses power. *It moves people's minds.*"

"It *is* a magic language," Daphna whispered.

Dex offered no comment. His thoughts soared.

"I'm not sure the word 'magic' does it justice," Ruby replied, "but it'll do. Knowledge of the First Tongue gives one the power to do virtually anything. It is a great and terrible thing. Fortunately, the language was lost, as they say, in the sands of time."

"But it's not real, is it?" Daphna asked. Despite everything they'd already seen, she just wasn't ready to accept this.

"Oh, it is real, Daphna," Ruby assured. "It is real."

"But, how do you know all this?"

"Well, I'm not as young as I look," was Ruby's odd reply. She brushed back her white hair a bit and touched her intricately etched cheek. "Believe it or not," she continued, "before the First Tongue vanished, words of power rolled quite fluently off this tongue."

She paused a moment, then added, "As they did your mother's."

a troublesome rash

Awestruck, the twins gaped at Ruby Scharlach, their suddenly unfathomably old host.

"At some point in history, children," she said, "humans learned to speak the First Tongue. How this came to pass is unknown, though there is an ancient myth that God himself read from a book containing this language when he created the world, but that later the book was lost, or stolen, and that is how the words of power reached Mankind. You are probably familiar with the story of Prometheus, who stole fire from the gods and gave it to Man. The expression 'tongues of fire' may actually connect the two. There are many variations of the theme."

Daphna was jolted. Were they now talking about *God*? This was not a subject she'd ever given much thought to before. *Any* thought, actually.

"Can—can *that* be true?" she stuttered.

"Useless to speculate," Ruby answered, brushing the topic aside. "What we do know is that the results were disastrous, though not immediately so. When people first learned the language, they used it to fuel great leaps forward in every field of human endeavor: agriculture, navigation, astronomy and the like. But soon enough, inevitably some might say, the words of power were used as weapons. Arguments previously settled, however unsatisfactorily, escalated rapidly into outright war. Entire populations were destroyed, and many civilizations were woefully stunted. Perhaps it was fortunate that the First Tongue was very difficult to master. The words of power were not easy to pronounce, you must understand. People don't develop the capacity to speak, or even hear, the words until the age of thirteen."

"Wait a minute," Daphna said. Her mind was whirling with this staggering new conception of history, but something suddenly clicked for her. "Yesterday," she said, "when I was spying on Rash and my father, it looked like Rash was mouthing silent words at him—and whatever he was doing was making my dad act really strange. I was twelve yesterday! And today, when he had me in his cubby I could hear the weird words he was mumbling to make me do what he wanted. And I'm thirteen today! He's been waiting for thirteen years to be able to control me—I mean, I guess, one of us. He isn't hypnotizing people!" she realized. "Rash speaks the First Tongue!"

Ruby shook her head. "Thankfully, Asterius can by no means speak the First Tongue," she said, "but yes, he has managed to acquire some words of power over the years."

"That's why he collects books on magic!" Dexter announced.

Ruby nodded, then continued with her story. "Because the First Tongue was so difficult to speak," she explained, "people began to neglect and mispronounce it, and in their foolishness, it seemed the words were failing them. Eventually, the language was forgotten by all but a few who retained it only in part, and they were regarded with fear and suspicion for the meager powers they possessed. Some were called devils or witches. A good number were killed, and in terrible ways, as you probably know. As you might expect, this caused many to give up their knowledge out of fear for their lives, and so the number of people who knew any part of it dwindled further still. You see, children, ignorance in all forms spreads faster than fire, and soon enough, even the very *idea* of the First Tongue was lost except in various forms of legend and myth."

"Wait, but not everyone forgot the language," Dex assumed. "What about you and our mom?"

"Several thousand years ago," Ruby said, "the thirty-six most intelligent thirteen-year-old children in the world were identified and invited to a secret academy. Your mother and I were among these children."

"The most intelligent children in the whole *world*?" Dex asked. "How did they manage that?"

"It was a mysterious processs," Ruby admitted. "I can only tell you that in my case, our teacher asked me to solve a difficult riddle. When I succeeded, he ruffled my hair and said I'd been selected. Our parents were told we'd be trained to become peacemakers among the nations. What they weren't told was that we'd become so by mastering the First Tongue. When our families departed, our teacher told us the truth: he'd discovered the language in an old book, but was too old and weak to make use of it. He'd decided to recruit and train us so that together we could bring, in his words, Heaven to Earth.

"But it was no easy task. Our teacher

never gave voice to the words himself, but rather left us to puzzle each one out for ourselves. It took nearly a year for us to master the very first word, but it was critical, for it enabled us to prolong our lives. If it took us ten thousand years to accomplish our task, our teacher was willing to wait."

"You mean," Daphna gasped, "a word for *immortality*?"

Ruby shook her head again. "No," she said. "That is the one word of power not in the book. Our word prolonged our lives prodigiously, but as you can see, time, even for us, is limited."

"Rash was one of the kids, too!" Dexter declared.

"Indeed," Ruby confirmed. "During our many years of study, he plotted a rebellion. He secretly won over all but nine of us—the Nine we were later called. His plan was to use the First Tongue to enslave the world. And now I can only assume he had the idea of training you—the surely talented children of one of us—to do it for him all these life-times later."

This struck the twins hard. Phrases like "enslave the world," were only for stories. They both had the same feeling just then—that they'd gotten themselves into something way over their heads.

"But you won. The Nine won, right?" Daphna knew it had to be that way.

"Indeed," Ruby confirmed. "We prevailed in what was known as the War of Words. All of Asterius' co-conspirators were crushed, all but Asterius himself because he was the most skillful among us. We did, however, manage to seal him in a stone cell after defeating him. Afterward, the Nine formed a Council because we had some terrible thinking to do. We'd lost so much, you see. Our teacher's dream was destroyed."

"What happened to him?" Dex asked.

"It is my personal belief that Asterius killed him because he disappeared the day the War began—and later we learned that

Asterius had his book. We never heard from him again."

"How did Rash get away?" asked Daphna.

"After much deliberation, the Council reached a difficult decision," Ruby explained. "This was that the First Tongue was best forgotten. We brought Asterius before us and told him we would use a word of Forgetting to wipe the words of power from our memories and then set him free. He agreed, and so we immediately began the ceremony on the misty mountaintop where we met."

"He was lying," Dex predicted.

"Yes. But fortunately one among us found him out. Her name was Sophia Logos. You see, as the word of Forgetting was taking effect, she used a word of Insight still within her mind's eye to inspect Asterius' heart. She was nearly as skillful as he. Sophia perceived his final scheme, then acted swiftly and with cunning. As the final few words of power drifted from us all, she grasped one last word and used it the best way she could. It was a word of Changing, and she directed it at the book she realized was hidden in the folds of Asterius' robe."

"He was going to try to learn the First Tongue again!" Daphna shouted. "And then he'd be the only one—"

Ruby nodded.

"What happened when he realized what Sophia did?" Dexter asked.

"When the Forgetting was complete," said Ruby, "Asterius found his book contained pages that changed—the words on the pages, changing from this to that, sometimes quickly, sometimes slowly, but forever changing."

Now Daphna leapt to her feet, nearly spilling her tea. "That's why he made me keep reading the first page, to see if anything changed! That's why he got so excited when I misread a word! But—*they are*! Some of the words *are* moving! I thought I was just carsick!" Daphna paused a moment, thinking.

"But—my dad, when he brought the book to Rash—wouldn't he have mentioned it if the words were actually moving?"

Ruby did not look encouraged. "It is likely," she said, "that at most times, it looks like an ordinary, if very strange, book."

"How did it get lost?" Dexter asked.

"When Asterius realized it might take centuries for the First Tongue to reappear on its pages," Ruby explained, "he went into a rage. First, he dashed the book to the ground. Then he attempted to pull it to pieces, and finally hurled it off the cliff. The book fell many hundreds of feet into a river dotted with boats. It was impossible to see whether it landed in the water or on some craft that took it to places unknown, though it soon became obvious that the latter is what occurred."

"How did you know?" Daphna asked, sitting back down.

"We knew the book was not destroyed because, as time passed, we began to notice that certain common folk throughout the world were developing modest powers. The book was making its way here and there, revealing at times some lesser words of power, but no instructions on how to pronounce them of course. People tried to use them to change base metals to gold, or tell the future from the stars. Some fashioned themselves into magicians and performed tricks for money; others became master thieves. Some were noble enough to cure the sick.

"But once in a while, a commoner found a truly dangerous word and used it to gain extraordinary power over their fellow men, setting themselves up as great leaders and putting their people's collective energies toward evil ends. Thankfully, this was rare, and the words eventually failed the tyrants.

"Consequently, the Council agreed that keeping an eye on Asterius was less important than finding that book. After all, he no longer knew the language any better than we did. I agreed to continue monitoring him alone, and the rest of the Council split up to track news of magical events around the world.

"Since then, we've lost contact with one another. I fear all the other Councilors have perished, for as I've said, none of us is immortal. Children," Ruby said, "we must get that book before it's too late. It seems I represent the Council alone. I am counting on you both, and I do not exaggerate when I say the fate of the world hangs in the balance."

Simultaneously, the twins swallowed lumps in their throats. They remained silent a moment before a question occurred to Dexter.

"Ruby," he said softly, "our Mom—you said you knew her by another name. What was it?"

"Why, haven't you guessed?" Ruby asked, looking surprised but smiling. "It was Sophia Logos of course."

167

bigger than him

Brother and sister sat silently, attempting to take in this latest bombshell.

Finally, Daphna asked, "When Rash read that article, about our mom, why did he think it was a Councilor who died?"

"Because of where it happened," Ruby answered. "That remote area in Turkey—those caves; they were very near where we were trained. But he couldn't have known it was your mother. She wasn't using her real name, and even a photo wouldn't have mattered. Living this long changes you profoundly. Unless they kept in touch, none of the Councilors would recognize each other after so—"

Ruby stopped short. The fire alarm was suddenly blaring in the hall. The twins stood up, frightened.

"Probably nothing," Ruby said, "but we better go." She rose and led the twins out of her room and toward the emergency stairwell directly across the hall. Daphna made a mad dash for it, hoping to avoid an encounter with the Seven Dwarves. It was a good thing, too, because out of the corner of her eye, she saw Mr. Dwyfan and Mrs. Tapi puzzling over the fire alarm box in front of the lounge. They seemed baffled, as if it were a piece of technology they'd never encountered before.

On the stairs, Daphna, Dex and Ruby ran into a group of eight rehab patients getting in some exercise. Each had some sort of wrap or sling or brace on one limb or another, and they were all clutching the railings, perspiring heavily. With the alarm, everyone was trying to reverse course all at once, so it was impossible to get around them. Further confusion ensued when, moments later, dozens more old people entered the stairs, both behind and in front.

It took a while for a slow moving mass to begin heading for the lobby, but no one seemed particularly worried, which Daphna thought was typical. In fact, the only thing she could hear was grumbling about how much everyone was being put out. When the crowd finally reached the first floor, a wedge formed separating Dexter, Daphna and Ruby. Daphna tried to push her way forward, but it was impossible.

"Where's the fire, young lady?!" someone demanded.

Daphna huffed, but didn't push any further. She had to inch her way into the lobby, where there was near pandemonium as nurses and visitors scrambled to evacuate the rehabilitation patients, many of whom were in wheelchairs or on crutches.

"False Alarm! False Alarm!" someone was shouting. It was Evelyn Idun. "We can all go back to our rooms in a few minutes!" she called. No one seemed to be paying her any mind.

After a short but panicked search, Daphna found Dex, and they forged a circuitous course through the grousing crowd. They looked for Ruby, desperate for more information, but with no luck.

A hand grabbed Daphna by the shoulder. "Daphna, honey!" It was Evelyn, appearing out of nowhere. "Oh, sweetie!" she said, "I'm so glad I caught you. A boy came here, *really* big, with dark glasses and an awfully pale face. He said he had to find you right away. He said there was some kind of emergency. He looked dreadfully upset. Since I never saw you come back down, I sent him up to the lounge, but I guess he missed you."

Daphna didn't waste a second replying. Talking more to Ruby would have to wait. She and Dex frantically wove their way outside, barely managing to avoid trampling a little old lady and her walker along the way.

Once outside, they sprinted off without looking back.

Dex, running ahead of his sister, reached

home first. He flew down the driveway and rounded behind the house, but he pulled up at the back door. Loud voices were audible from the kitchen: his father and Latty, back from the hospital, were arguing strenuously.

Moments later, Daphna came tearing toward him. Dex intercepted her and led her into the garage.

"What's going on? Dad's home!" Daphna said, pointing at the car in the driveway.

"I can see that," Dex said tersely. "Let's wait and see what's going on."

Daphna nodded. She'd lost her head for a moment. When she finally caught her breath, she said, "I guess Emmet finally figured out we stole the ledger."

Dex nodded. "But how would he know where you were?"

"Rash I suppose. Dad told him I read to old folks at the local home."

"Emmet probably pulled the alarm so he could grab us without making a scene."

"Where was he then?" Daphna asked.

"Dex, he probably wants to kill us. He seems as obsessed with killing someone as Rash is about this book." Then something occurred to her. "He said Rash doesn't hypnotize him, but maybe he just doesn't know it. Maybe we can snap him out of it!"

Dex couldn't process this. All he could say was, "*Mom!*"

Daphna didn't reply, but the look of amazement on her face was enough to show her brother the incredible news was striking her again as well. The pair paused for a moment, finally able to reflect on what they'd learned from Ruby. Their very own mother had been on the Council, and she was the one who'd foiled Rash's plans. She'd been thousands of years old! It was still too much to comprehend, so Dex and Daphna fell into a long, thoughtful silence.

After a minute, Dex heard himself say, "About Wren and Teal, I—"

Daphna blinked at her brother, instantly pale. She couldn't handle this right now.

When did Dexter take it upon himself to ruin her life? It was clear she was the real loser in the family, and now he was going to lord it over her, probably forever.

"I made that up," Dex admitted. "I didn't really see them in the park."

"What?"

"I'm sorry. I was just being a jerk. I never saw either one of them."

Daphna's ears went red. "But—but—" She searched her brother's eyes but couldn't detect even a trace of insincerity. "Thanks," she whispered.

Dex had no idea why he'd decided to admit this just then, or what to say next, but it didn't matter because at that moment the back door of the house burst open. Milton was struggling to get outside with Latty trying to restrain him. The twins tiptoed to the garage door.

"Get back to bed!" Latty demanded. "You heard what the doctor said. You're worn out! And the kids are missing! It's their birthday, Milton! We need to have a proper party!"

"Unhand me, woman!" Milton ordered, trying to scrape Latty off like a stubborn burr. At the same time, he was trying to get into an overcoat. It was drizzling again.

"You're not even dressed!" Latty shouted. She was right. Milton was in his flannel pajamas.

"I am going to get that book!" Milton wailed, evidently unconcerned with his choice of outfit. "Quartich thinks he's got a copy. Do you understand me?!"

"Let me go, then!! I'll get it for you! And I can look for the kids—!"

"Not bloody likely! Now, get out of my way!"

Defeated, Latty relinquished her grip, then stormed back inside the house. Milton moved toward the car, but couldn't get in before she reappeared with her shawl.

"You're out of your mind, Latona! I do not require a chaperone!" Milton slammed his door and started the car. Latty's reply was lost as she climbed in.

Given no alternative, he raced off with her inside, squealing the tires on the driveway as he went.

"Shouldn't we have tried to stop him?" Daphna asked.

"I don't think we could've," said Dex. "And it wasn't worth letting Latty get her hands on us."

"Hey!" Daphna said, "we can call this Quarts guy and tell him not to sell the book to Dad!"

"Quartich," Dex corrected, "but I think we ought to forget about it."

"What? He's going to get that book right now!"

"I think we should stop bothering with Dad," said Dex. "This is bigger than him. We need to solve the real problem once and for all."

"What do you mean?"

"I think we should do what Mom and all

the other Councilors were trying to do. We should destroy that book."

Daphna agreed immediately. That was exactly what they should do. "Without that book of nonsense," she conceded, "that Latin book's no use to Rash, and neither is Dad. But how can we do it, Dex?"

"That other book," Dex said. An idea was germinating. "I mean that Latin dictionary we have. Didn't you say it looks just like the nonsense book?"

"Great idea!" Daphna cried.

The twins rushed back into the house. Daphna sprinted to the office for the dictionary, then met Dex in the kitchen. He'd grabbed a box of extra long fireplace matches and had one already burning. Slowly, Daphna moved the edges of the book's pages over the flame. Each time the fire took hold, Dex blew it out. The process took about fifteen minutes, but soon enough the pages were charred all around.

Daphna opened a drawer and took out

Latty's best knife.

"Let me do that!" Dexter said. Daphna handed him the knife, and Dex, embarrassed only slightly, proceeded to gash the front and back covers. It was an intensely pleasurable experience.

"It was warped, too," Daphna said, taking the dictionary back before Dex hacked it to shreds. She placed it in the sink and ran water over it. "I can't believe what we're doing to this poor book," she lamented. "It's probably worthless now."

When the book was soaked, Daphna put it into the microwave. She set it for three minutes and beeped it on.

"I guess that's the closest thing to a birthday cake that's gonna get cooked around here today," Dex said. But then he turned back to Daphna, who was already looking at him with eyes asparkle.

"Presents!" they cried.

misreading

The twins dashed toward their father's room with nothing but the image of brightly wrapped gifts in their minds. Once inside, they threw themselves onto the floor on either side of the bed.

Their eyes met across the empty space below.

"What are we doing?" Daphna sighed, but her embarrassment was no match for her disappointment.

"Yeah," Dex agreed, "this is an emergency, and we're acting like little kids." But he couldn't hide the disappointment in his voice, either.

"Dex," Daphna said. It was weird talking across the floor under a bed, but she didn't get up. "I—about Ruby—and you," she said. "I—I'm—Hold on, I found something." Daphna picked something up off the floor, a slip of paper maybe. She slid out from under the bed and sat up. "Dex!"

Dexter looked up over the bed to find his sister holding out a hundred dollar bill.

"C'mere," Daphna urged. "Look!" She was pointing at something on her side of the mattress. Dex climbed over the bed. There was another bill, a twenty, trapped against the mattress by the bedskirt.

Dex and Daphna attacked, ripping the blankets and sheet from the bed. There, running along the length of the mattress, was a zipper. A clutch of bills poked out where it wasn't fully closed. Holding her breath, Daphna eased the zipper open.

The twins gasped. The mattress was stuffed with cash, bills of all denominations. Handfuls fell to the floor, along with something else: a bright yellow card.

Grinning, Daphna grabbed it up. But then she read how it was labeled. "That's bizarre," she said. "Look."

Dex looked, but he didn't respond. Instead, he turned his attention back to all that money. What did it mean?

"That's totally weird, don't you think?" Daphna said. "I'll bet he was hiding it and forgot! And there's no way he wrote this, anyway. Latty must've done it for him!"

"Why do you say that?" Dex asked, though with little interest. All that money—

"When has Dad ever referred to us that way?"

"What way?"

"Look!" Daphna demanded. "Would Dad ever write, 'For My Beloved Children on their Thirteenth Birthday'? Hardly."

"Doesn't sound like him," Dex admitted, ignoring his sister's tone. "Open it."

Disgusted, Daphna tore into the envelope. Inside was a folded sheet of paper with something typed on it. She smoothed it flat and began looking it over, but a moment later, she jerked her head up at Dex with saucered eyes.

"*What?*" Dex asked. "What is it?"

"It's from Mom," was Daphna's somber response. She read it aloud:

My Dearest Children,

I am writing to you now, just minutes before I leave on a most unexpected journey.

For so very long I have been searching for a book. This search has consumed my time in this world and denied me what I truly seek, what we all seek: to live, to love. May you never know loneliness like I have known. May you be surrounded by those who love you all the days of your lives. How blessed you are to have each other!

I broke my word, children, and renounced the search. I found Love. Uttering those two small, simple words, "I do," set me free. And now I have you and my joy knows no bounds.

Only now it seems that the book may be within reach. I am going to find out. I expect the best, but something I cannot put my finger on worries me, and so I must write you this note.

There is a man, Asterius Rash, who will go to any length to find this dangerous book, including murdering children. Should you ever cross his path, run! Under no circumstances should you have anything to do with this vile man.

It is my profound wish that you never read this note, for if you do, it will be because I am gone. I love you so much. I must admit I did not think it possible that you two could ever be. Two

little miracles! Latona did me
the greatest favor in my long
life when she encouraged me to
try for you. I need you both
to know how much I love you,
how much I will always, always
love you.

There was more, but Daphna stopped
reading and dropped her head. "Here," she
choked, holding the sheet out to Dex, "I can't
go on." She looked up when Dex didn't take
the paper. "Dex, I can't do it. I just can't."

"Of course you can," Dex said.

"Please, it's too hard."

"Oh, come on, Daphna. Just read the
stupid thing."

"I can't, Dexter!" Daphna shouted.
"Can't you just do me a simple favor for
once without turning everything into a huge
war?!"

For a moment, Dex offered no reply.
Then he said, in a slow, measured voice, "I

can't read it for you, Daphna. *Okay?*"

"*Why not?!* It's not like it's in French! I'm sorry—look—I'm really sorry I didn't know about you getting help for school and all that. I'm sorry I always say you don't care, but it's really your fault for keeping it all a secret and acting like—"

"You don't get it," Dex interrupted. "For once in your life, you just don't get it."

Dex's voice sounded distant, like someone else was talking through his mouth. It was unsettling.

"*What? I don't get what?*" Daphna asked.

"I can't read it for you, Daphna. I can't read it for you because—"

"*What already?*"

"I can't *read*, Daphna."

There, he said it. Dex had no idea why now, after so long, at this time, in this place. But he said it.

"Oh, my God," was Daphna's reply. In a single dizzying moment, she reconsidered a lifetime. A thousand little things Dex had

185

said and done since they were little suddenly shifted meaning—suddenly *had* meaning. He'd never help look for street signs in the car. He'd never look at menus in restaurants. He'd never look up a phone number or take down a message. And all the trouble he got into at school for refusing to participate in class!

Daphna knew without any doubt whatsoever that it was true. Her brother couldn't read. But at the same time, she didn't understand how it could possibly be. "But— But—" Daphna sputtered.

"Memorizing," Dex said, looking at the floor.

"What?"

"I memorize everything." Dexter understood Daphna's confusion precisely because it was his life's mission—since the moment when he was five and realized something was drastically wrong with him—to make sure she, and everyone else, was at best confused about him. If the world had to think he was lazy or ignorant, so be it, because it was far better to look like you won't than you can't.

"I memorize everything," he repeated. "If the teacher says it once, I know it. I get books on tape from the library, or I listen when other kids read. Ruby doesn't even know. She liked reading my books to me, but on tests you have to read something you've never seen before. I fail all my tests."

"Dex—I—I—"

"I can write some words," Dex said. His eyes were still fixed on the floor. "I don't know how, but I can. They're like pictures I guess—short words anyway. I make the ones I can't do so sloppy that no one can tell. I used to pretend I didn't know answers in class because teachers start asking questions when you know everything you're supposed to but then bomb all the tests." Dex paused as a pronounced shudder passed through him.

Finally, he looked directly at Daphna, who saw his eyes were filling. "It's like I've got wires crossed up in my brain or something. When I look at a page of words, all I see is—"

The back door banged open.

"*OH, IT'S GONNA BE YOU!*" Emmet screamed. "*IT'S GONNA BE BOTH OF YOU!*"

Dexter sprang to his feet, his face stony and alert. "Shh," he whispered, kicking the money under the bed as best he could. He was amazed at the calm he felt.

"Listen," Dex said, hustling his sister into their father's closet. "There's only one way he's going to leave without you, and that's if you stay in here! I have a plan." Dex said this because he did. "I only hope Dad gets that Latin book to Rash soon!" Daphna was too afraid to respond, and Dex didn't explain. They could hear Emmet crashing his way downstairs.

"When we're gone," Dex whispered, "get the book out of the microwave and follow us. Go down through the trapdoor to the loft, but be careful. Aim for the line of light at the center, okay?"

Daphna managed a nod.

"Just make sure you figure out a way to get me our book—and cause a distraction when—"

Stomping feet were just outside the room. Dex shut the closet door and had only just turned around when Emmet raged into the room.

"*YOU!*" Emmet screamed, his glasses once again askew, his pale cheeks flushed with fury. "*WHERE'S MY LEDGER?!* Do you know what it's like to search through five hundred thousand books?! If I ever get my hands on that—that lying—she's dead! Both of you are dead!"

"I have no idea what you're talking about, Emmet," Dex said. Daphna thought he sounded rather composed through the door, and that gave her some comfort, though her nerves were raw. She unconsciously squeezed the note from her mother in her fist.

"Oh, really?" Emmet sneered. Daphna heard a sudden rush of movement, then an awful grunt. A body hit the floor. She bit her lip and tasted blood.

"I don't know what you're talking about," Dex groaned. "*I mean it.*" This was met by another sudden movement and a gruesome thwack. Dex cried out in pain. Violence of any sort nauseated Daphna. She couldn't bear much more of this.

"I'm telling you, Emmet," Dex grunted, "I have no idea where my sister is. We hate each other."

There was silence in room. Daphna held her breath.

"Let's go then," Emmet finally snarled.

Daphna winced at the groan Dex made when he was hauled to his feet. It sounded like he was dragged from the room.

When she was sure she was alone, Daphna crept out of the closet, tottering on her feet. With quaking hands, she stuffed the money on the floor back into the mattress and hastily remade the bed. Afterward, she looked at her mother's face framed on her father's wall. "I'm sorry," she whispered, then ran to the kitchen. First, she threw up in the sink, but once that was done, she opened the microwave and took out the now badly disfigured but mostly dry book.

One deep breath, and then she started out after her brother.

the old switcheroo

All concept of time was lost to Daphna the moment she stepped out of the house, but she noticed that scenery passed as she ran along under the gathering gloom of the late afternoon skies.

At some point, the ABC appeared.

There was no sign of Dex or Emmet, so Daphna headed down the concrete stairs leading behind the store. Halfway down she heard a car screech to a halt on the street. She stopped.

Car doors opened, then slammed. Then Latty's voice. Daphna strained to hear, worried sick about what might be happening to Dex.

"Will you or will you not go straight home after you've delivered it?" Latty demanded.

"I will," Milton replied.

"I'll wait right here," Latty said, but then changed her mind. "No! I'll just run quickly down to the toy store. It's your children's birthday, Milton!"

Daphna snuck back up the steps and peeked around the corner. When she saw Latty hurry off, she leapt out. "Dad!" she cried. Fortunately, Milton was just standing at the door holding a book in one hand and worrying his ring on the other. He blinked at her when he realized who she was.

"Daphna!" he said. "Are you here to help Mr. Rash again?"

"I—ah—" Daphna had no idea what to say. She was holding the Latin dictionary behind her back. "That—that book—" she managed, pointing to the one in her father's hand.

"Yes, Mr. Rash is simply desperate for this odd thing. So if you'll excuse me, I'll just—"

"Don't, Dad! He's making you—" Daphna

cut herself off. Dex said he wanted the Latin book to get to Rash. Only he didn't say why. Daphna knew she'd been wrong about practically everything she ever thought about her brother, but that didn't suddenly turn him into a reliable person, did it? Was this the time to start trusting him? *What should I do?* She decided. She'd trust Dex for now, and she suddenly had an idea of how to get the phony Book of Nonsense at least close to him.

"Actually, Dad, I need your advice," said Daphna. "I'm selling my first book." She produced the mutilated Latin dictionary from behind her back. "I know it's all beaten up—"

"*Is that the book?*" Milton yelped, snatching it away. Daphna was shocked by his ferocity. But as he flipped through it, she looked at his shrouded eyes and realized how deeply he was under Rash's sway. When he realized it wasn't the book, Milton sighed mightily.

Daphna exhaled. He hadn't recognized it. "I've got to run, Dad," she lied. "Can you just

see if Mr. Rash will buy that one? Thanks!"
She turned and walked away, shaken.

A few paces off, Daphna stopped, turned
and saw Milton enter the store. Then she ran
back to the steps, but stopped once again with
a hand on the rusty railing, breathing heavily,
weighed down by second thoughts. Had she
done the right thing? Daphna was desperate
now to make sure Dex was okay, yet she felt a
terrible foreboding about her father.

Suddenly, Emmet's voice exploded
through the open front entrance. "*NOW GET
LOST!*" he barked.

Again, the sound of violence. With her
heart in her throat, Daphna once again peeked
around the edge of the building, this time to
see her father stumbling backwards through
the door. His heels clipped the sidewalk, and
his legs buckled. He fell, twisting, and landed
on his side, hitting the concrete with a horrify-
ing crunch. His head hit next. Milton let out a
cry on impact, then went silent.

Emmet stood over him with teeth bared.

Witnessing this paralyzed Daphna, but to her indescribable relief, Milton moved, though feebly, and started saying something she couldn't hear. The book Daphna had given him was still in his hand. Emmet held the one he'd brought.

"Help!" someone screamed. It was Latty. "Help! Police! Help!"

Emmet turned and tried to see where the voice came from. Whether he could tell or not, he threw his head back and shouted, "Call whoever you want! *WE'RE CLOSED FOREVER!*"

Then he looked down at Milton and hissed, "You come back here, and you'll be the one for sure." He leaned over, ripped the book Milton still held out of his hand, then stepped back into the store. The door slammed and bolted behind him.

Latty was there now, on her knees next to Milton, who was bent in a heap, quietly muttering something unintelligible. Daphna forced herself to turn and rush down the steps. What she just saw simply didn't happen. Drenched again by fear for her brother, Daphna found the ladder on the far side and scrambled up to the roof.

The trap door was lying open.

Without allowing herself to think, Daphna climbed onto the ladder.

The first few rungs were no problem, but halfway down there came a long, unnerving creak. Daphna stopped, but the creaking did not. Rather, it got louder and louder until the right side of the ladder came free from the wall. Desperately, Daphna clutched the handholds as it swung slowly out over the loft. She tried not to move, or even breathe, but the ladder drifted back again, and it swung slowly to and fro before finally settling perpendicular to the wall. Daphna had no choice but to climb down on it the way it was.

The ladder creaked this way and that with every shift of weight, but Daphna managed to get a foot on the loft. Her second foot had only just touched down when the ladder came off the wall entirely. It was heavy; Daphna barely managed to lower it to the floor without dropping it.

Now there was no way out, but that was just one more thing not to think about. Instinctively, Daphna got down on her stomach, coughed at her first inhale of dust, then headed toward the thin line of light, aiming for the middle of the store.

The decaying loft was almost putrid, but Daphna pushed through the stifling rot without hesitation, and before she knew it, she was approaching the dimly outlined edge. The sound of an angry voice directed her to her left. Moments later, she was there, right above it. It was Rash. He was talking to Dex, who was seated across the desk from him. Relief washed over Daphna, but it quickly dawned on her that she had no idea what she was supposed to do now that she was there.

"For the last time, boy," Rash was demanding, "I am out of patience! *Read the page!*" Dex sat in the same chair Daphna had on her visit, and Rash held the book open in front of him the way he had for her. Two new candles burned beside his elbow. Dex did not obey, and it was obvious why, at least to Daphna. He had his fingers jammed into his ears. Dex was also anxiously peering up toward the loft, clearly waiting for her.

Waiting for what? Daphna gripped the floor as her nerves threatened to overcome her. A sliver peeled up under her fingers. She stared at it a moment, then thought: *perfect*, and tossed it down toward Dex. It bounced off of his elbow. Ever so slightly, he nodded.

"Enough of this—*EMMET*!" Rash fumed, shattering his cane on the desk once and for all. "Emmet, you half-wit! Get over here!"

Emmet called out from somewhere, though what he was saying wasn't clear until he was just outside the cubby. "I got the book! I got the book!" he was shouting. Daphna hadn't noticed until then that there was no longer an entranceway into the little six-sided room. Shelves had enclosed the space entirely.

Rash muttered a word, and the shelves swung open to allow Emmet inside. After another word, the shelf swung shut. Daphna shivered, wondering what other words of power Rash had learned.

"I know you got the book, you ignoramus!" Rash spat. "Hold on to it. I will need it momentarily. But first I must settle a problem. Dexter here seems somehow immune to my—I am impressed, but extremely put out. My words seem to have no—but now I see. How clever," he sighed. "Emmet, please remove Dexter's fingers from his ears."

Dex didn't need to hear this to size-up the new situation. He lowered his hands by himself.

"Dexter Wax, you naughty boy," Rash scolded, though not without amusement in his voice. "You and your sister have been far more trouble than you're worth. Perhaps

I'll pass on my usual methods of persuasion in favor of a more traditional technique. Emmet, the next time Mr. Wax here refuses a request, please break eight of his fingers. We might need the thumbs later."

"Yes, Sir!" Emmet promised. "It's gonna be him, isn't it?" Daphna gasped at this, but was not heard. "Oh, got this, too," Emmet added, putting the ruined Latin dictionary on the desk.

Despite the ice creeping through her veins, Daphna allowed herself a brief smile. *It worked.* She'd gotten the book there. Both books were there. Now, what in the world did Dex think he was going to do?

Rash felt for the new book and took it into his hands. He seemed intrigued, but only until he'd felt through a few pages, after which he tossed it on the floor.

"Your father was going to try a little sleight-of-hand, it seems," Rash said. "The poor man was starting not to trust me. Imagine that. Now, Dexter, you and I will be going away together very soon. But first, I need the use of your eyes. And thanks to your fool of a father, I will have them. Emmet, do your best to scan the pages of *Videre Per Alterum*. Afterward, Dexter will be giving a reading."

Daphna nearly cried out. What had Dex been thinking? Of course Rash would ask him to read, and when Dex told him he couldn't, he probably wouldn't believe him. Rash would probably forget breaking his fingers and just have Emmet break his neck—and then it would be her turn, and there she was, a sitting duck with no way out! Or, did it matter that Dex couldn't read?!

Reeling, Daphna's mind threatened to close down on her entirely as Emmet began flipping through the pages. *Dexter never thinks things through—like throwing away that ledger!* She should have come herself and left *him* in the closet!

Wait! She was supposed to cause a distraction.

"There it is!" Rash cried. "*STOP!*"

Daphna panicked. *A distraction!* But what could she do, lying there in ten tons of dust?

The dust!

Daphna scooped up a handful and dropped it over Rash.

"What's this?" he demanded, wiping at his head and beard.

Daphna pushed more dust over the edge. It fell like dirty snow on top of Rash, who raised his arms to ward it off.

"Emmet, you cretin!" he bellowed, "the loft!"

Emmet looked up, straining his eyes.

Rash waved his arms wildly as the dust continued to fall.

Dexter saw his chance. He leaned forward and closed Rash's precious, but now unattended book. Then he slipped it into the front pocket of his sweatshirt. Daphna intensified her storm, sweeping sheets of dust down into the cubby, one after another, with everything she had. Slowly, painfully slowly, Dex bent down to the floor and picked up the Latin dictionary. He laid it open on the desk. Then he sat back.

"It's the girl!" Rash roared.

"Yeah!"

"Get her down here!"

Daphna stopped. There was no point in continuing, and any fleeting sense of success evaporated. What were they going to do now? Didn't Dexter just see that Rash could tell the books apart?

"Enough of this," said Rash. "Daphna, come down right now, or I'll have Emmet tear your brother's head off."

"Don't hurt him! I'm coming!"

"Don't!" Dex cried, but Daphna ignored him. She turned around and lowered her feet over the edge of the loft until they reached the top of the shelving unit directly below. It was only a foot or so down. From there, she sat on her behind to consider her next move, but Emmet grabbed her by the ankle and yanked her down. Then he shoved her into a chair next to Dex.

"Got her," Emmet said. "Please let it be—"

"Excellent, boy," Rash interrupted. "I believe your time is nearly here."

Emmet seemed too thrilled to do anything but grin, so Dex took advantage of the moment.

"You're making a big mistake," he warned. It was a long shot, but maybe their only shot.

"Indeed, Mr. Wax?" Rash ran a gnarled hand through his dust-encrusted beard. "Do tell."

"Emmet wouldn't hurt a fly," Dex said. "He knows you've been hypnotizing him."

"That's right," Daphna put in. "He knows you kidnapped him. He knows he used to have a big family with lots of brothers and sisters."

Rash's response to this was another laughing fit.

"The Wax Twins!" he croaked. "You entertain me to no end, you arrogant little twits! You know nothing! There's never been a need to, as you say, *hypnotize* any of them. I purposely pick out the most stupid looking ones at the—but *ENOUGH OF THIS*!"

"It's too late, *Asterius*," Dexter pressed. "We called the police and told them everything."

"Rousing," Rash replied, "but I've had my fill of your nonsense."

"Our mother was Sophia Logos!" Daphna wailed.

This seemed to give Rash pause. His face went blank for a moment, but then he smiled. "Of course she was!" he laughed. "How positively poetic." Then he turned to Emmet and said, "I do still need your help, my boy. *EMMET!*"

"Yes! Yes, Sir," Emmet blurted. He sounded startled.

"Emmet, you are moments away from your destiny. I need but two new eyes, yet

206

here we have four. An embarrassment of riches! Which pair looks durable enough to spend a lifetime gazing into my precious book, assuming it is my precious book. If I'm wrong, then a serious change of plans will be necessary."

Terror swamped the twins. Did Rash just say what it sounded like? Emmet didn't hesitate for a second. "Make him do it!"

"Done," Rash replied. Then he slid his hands over the table until they found the book sitting there. He opened it to the first page and pushed it toward Dex. "A test run, Mr. Wax, if you don't mind." This time, he didn't hold onto it. He sat back as if getting comfortable for a show.

Daphna closed her eyes as her brother took up the book. They were both going to be killed, she was sure of it. She heard Dex's voice: "Sutro," he said, "Ibn lanik exo nadas circa earl." He paused, and Daphna opened her eyes, completely confused. What just happened? Dex couldn't read, and it wasn't even the right book!

Then she got it. His memory was that good, and he'd wanted it to come to this.

"Go on!" Rash ordered. "Go on!"

"I—I can't," Dex said. "The words, they're—they're—"

"What boy? What?"

"*They're moving!*"

Rash's face began to tremble. "Emmet!" he cried, "read that spell! The last line on that page you've got. *EMMET!*"

"Okay," Emmet finally answered, "where is it?"

"You dolt! Never mind, give it to the girl! It's only appropriate that she participate, anyway."

With his mouth in a cold, hard line, Emmet handed *Videre Per Alterum* to Daphna.

"To think, we could have avoided all these absurdities if you two hadn't taken my ledger," Rash sighed. "But, then, would we ever have had so much fun? Read me the last line, please. Just the first few words should be enough to jog my memory."

Daphna hesitated. She was going to refuse, but she glanced at Dex, who nodded his head, subtly. It was too late now not to trust him. She read the first part of the line, three words that sounded Chinese.

Rash became agitated as soon as she began. "Of course!" he hooted. "Of course! I have it now. Thank you. Emmet, take the book back." Daphna handed it over as Rash began intoning the words she'd read. He added a series of other, similar sounding words with his dead, cold eyes trained on Dex.

There was silence, and then Rash and Emmet and Dex were all rubbing their eyes.

Rash put his hands down and blinked at Dex, who was doing the same at him. The old man smiled wildly, exposing his rotten teeth. "Not such a handsome devil anymore, I see," he laughed.

Daphna realized he was seeing himself through her brother's eyes.

So that was it then.

"Look at the book, Dexter," Rash commanded.

"Don't do it!" Daphna couldn't watch this anymore. She tried to stand, but Emmet was suddenly behind her with his hands like vice-grips crushing her shoulders.

Slowly, Dexter lowered his eyes to the pages lying open in his hands.

walls fall

"Give it to me!" Rash screamed. He was struggling to his feet, erupting with delight.

Dex held the book out.

Daphna had no idea what had just happened. It seemed impossible.

"*THE BOOK!*" Rash exulted, "*AT LAST I FOUND IT!*" He lifted it up like a gladiator raising the severed head of a vanquished foe. A twisted grin contorted his face as he performed a gleeful dance behind his desk.

Daphna bulged her eyes at Dex, who bulged his eyes back, indicating that she should sit tight. What else could he do? They'd reached the end of his plan.

Finally, Rash finished his celebration and took his seat again. "You have pleased me, Dexter," he said, breathing heavily, "and so I will indeed choose you. It is time for us to go. If you are lucky, it won't take the rest of your life to find what I seek in these pages. You have many long years ahead of you, and my time is not up yet!" Rash leaned back like he'd just eaten a sumptuous feast.

"You'll note, dear children," he said, "that I am not completely without feeling. There is no need for Dexter to watch. It may scar. Emmet, my boy, at long last your time has come. Please take Ms. Wax out of the cubby and strangle her. Then go get the truck. We'll be leaving immediately."

Daphna didn't hear the last part of these instructions. She'd fainted dead away. Emmet let go of her shoulders, letting her hit the floor like a waterlogged rag doll.

Dexter threw himself at Emmet, but seconds later he was on the floor, too, with a split lip and a black eye. His sister lay next to him, already coming to. Dex tried to say something, anything, but he couldn't talk with so much blood in his mouth.

Daphna was being dragged to her feet. "Nooo!" she was pleading. Dex was too disoriented even to know where she was.

Rash muttered something. The shelves swung open.

"Please no!" Daphna implored.

Rash muttered again. The shelves closed. Dex had managed only to sit up in a spinning room. He heard his sister begging for her life, but then her voice was gone.

"We're alone," whispered Asterius Rash. He mumbled something, then said, "Take a seat, please, Dexter. Don't worry about your sister."

Dex had tried to put his fingers back in his ears, but he didn't have the strength. And now, suddenly, he didn't have the will either. He got on all fours and hauled himself back into the chair.

"You are mine," Rash cooed. "I am your master. How do you feel about that?"

"Sounds good, Mr. Rash," Dexter managed to say, and he meant it.

"Fabulous! Are you ready to go?"

"Ready, Mr. Rash."

"All right then. Let's just give Emmet another minute. Then we'll—"

Something slammed into the cubby. An entire shelf shook from the force of the blow.

"Emmet!" Rash howled, but the only answer was another terrific collision. The shelf shuddered, causing a look of rage and confusion on Rash's face. He clutched the book to his chest. "*EMMET!*" he demanded. "What's going on?"

CRASH!

Something rammed the shelves with incredible force. This time it was another unit, which shook ominously.

Someone, or something, was trying to get in. Rash shrieked a command, and the quaking shelves settled.

CRASH!

Another shelf jolted. Rash shrieked again, and again the shelf stabilized. Dex sat motionless through all this, dazed but feeling rather good.

An agonized wail sliced into the cubby then, followed by yet another crash. The shelf directly behind Rash tipped precariously forward, then teetered. It was going over!

Rash screamed at the shelf, but it was too late. The old man lunged from his seat just before the entire thing crashed over his desk.

On impact, books burst into the air, but Dex remained sitting calmly in his chair, both unfazed and, luckily, untouched. With mild interest, he noticed Emmet standing in place of the fallen shelves. He'd knocked down the wall of books and was preparing to do the same to another. Daphna was nowhere to be seen, but Dex wasn't worried about her.

"*AHHHH!*" Emmet screamed, ramming his bulk into the next shelf. This one came down easily.

"Move, boy!" Rash ordered. "Or you're going to get killed!" Dex dove from his chair, and before the third wall fell, he managed to crawl under Rash's desk.

"*AHHH!*" Emmet cried again.

CRASH!

Another wall fell.

Books were everywhere, and now there was smoke. Dexter definitely smelled smoke.

Fire!

Rash's candles had ignited the books. Within seconds, flames were swarming over the piles of old, brittle books strewn in all directions.

Dexter kicked debris from the opening under the desk and forced his way out into the store. How could the flames spread so quickly? Books looked as if they were spontaneously combusting. Smoke billowed, filling the air, and Dex couldn't keep it out of his lungs. But he had to find his master.

On a good day—on the best day—he'd have been lost quickly enough. In the stifling smoke and flames, Dex was lost instantaneously. Walls of flames turned him away from one path, then another and another. Choking, he staggered blindly among shelves, crashing into them here and there, knocking books free at every turn. Hurtling around a corner, Dex tripped, flew forward and landed flat on his chest. The air exploded out of him. His lungs felt like they'd been crushed. In the fetal position, he gasped for air. It was unbearable. It burned. But gradually, his breath returned.

Barely conscious, Dex got to his knees. The smoke and flames were gone. He was outside in the park, on the path, backed up against a tree. A ring of kids stood around him, pointing fingers and laughing. Dex swung at a boy with crazy red hair—was there a boy there? He missed and fell on his face. He got up, now with a large rock he'd grabbed. But it wasn't a rock—it was a book. Dexter threw it away. Emmet was there. What was he doing? He was talking to himself and throwing his shoulder against a set of bookshelves. But there were no bookshelves in the park. Then he disappeared into a cloud. When did it get so foggy in the park?

Dex resumed his stagger. He wheezed and gasped. He was lost, hopelessly lost. He was faltering, but found the strength to call out for his master. "Mr. Rash! Mr. Rash!"

It was hot, unreasonably hot. *Chaos!* Dexter's eyes burned. He could barely breathe. His throat felt scorched. Burning books were everywhere, everywhere. Where was he? "Mr. Rash! Mr. Rash!"

Dex fell to a knee, choking. The world began to fade like the background in a cartoon slowly being erased.

Hands grabbed, pulling him to his feet. Can't see. Can't *think*. Being rushed along. Left turns, right turns. They came too quickly to comprehend. The door! Outside! *Air!* At the urging of the hands that guided him, Dex stumbled across the street and collapsed on the sidewalk, coughing so hard he thought he'd loose his lungs. Sirens wailed in the distance.

"*Dex!*"

It was Daphna, her hair insane, her face blackened. Now she collapsed too, and brother and sister retched beside each other. The moment he thought he could, Dex tried to stand, but collapsed again calling, "Mr. Rash!"

"Dex!" Daphna said, looking into his hazy eyes. "He got you! He said you were going away with him! To be his new assistant!"

Dex blinked, confused.

"Emmet!" Daphna choked. "I figured it out! Rash gave it away!" She fell into a coughing fit, then gasped out the rest of her explanation. "Something about the way Rash said he 'picked' all his assistants made me think he might get them from orphanages. Emmet told me a lot of boys and girls were nice to him once, and that Rash told him it was only a dream. I was right! And he remembered!

"I told him Rash didn't have to hypnotize him. I mean, if you tell a kid his whole life he's a brainless animal who wants to kill someone—that's the same thing isn't it? His eyes got wide all of a sudden, and he let me go! Then his face went so sad. I—I don't know why—but I told him I knew he wasn't a bad person deep down, and then I—I hugged him. He looked at me all funny, and then he went berserk. *Look!*"

Dex, struggling to understand, looked back at the ABC. Somehow, Rash had made his way outside, too. He seemed unharmed, though he was hacking violently. His once-white beard was nearly black, and his robe was singed and smoking. The warehouse behind him was an inferno.

Rash looked around wildly, but then caught sight of himself from Dexter's eyes. "Thanks for showing me the way!" he thundered, laughing maniacally and patting his robe. He waved his precious book in the air. "I have all I need, Wax twits! And you can't hide from me, Dexter, unless you'd like to put your eyes out! There is nowhere you can go that I can't—"

Rash's eyes burst wide. Two arms, engulfed in flame, had grabbed him from behind. It was Emmet—Emmet on fire. With flames coiling and writhing over his entire body, he'd emerged from the shop behind Rash—a human figure of fire—and now he gripped his former master in a blazing bear hug.

Rash screamed, but Emmet simply lifted him off the ground like a toddler, turned and stepped back inside the store, which was no longer a store. It was mountain of fire. Seconds later, the front portion of the building collapsed.

"I've got the book!" Dex cried, pulling it free from his sweatshirt pocket.

Daphna saw that her brother's eyes were clear. "But how? What happ—? What should we do with it?"

"Ruby! She'll know what to do!"

"Go!" Daphna said. "I've got to see about Dad. I think he might be in the hospital."

Dexter nodded fearfully at this news. He clambered woozily to his feet, but a moment later, he regained his bearings. A moment after that he was sprinting all-out for the Multnomah Village Rest and Rehabilitation Home.

letters and numbers

As concerned for her father as she was, Daphna had to remain sitting on the sidewalk. She felt nauseated. Emmet really had been going to kill her. His huge, sweaty hands had been trembling with anticipation around her throat.

"You're dead now, girl," he'd hissed through that gash of a mouth as he dragged her through the store. Daphna had no doubt whatsoever that he would've gone through with it had he not let go of her neck to get a better grip.

"Orphanage!" she'd blurted, and it stopped him long enough for her to deliver her newly formed theory. Then the hug. She'd been seconds away from dying! *What did that mean?*

The sirens were getting closer now. Daphna got up and managed to pull herself together enough to run toward home, but after a train of emergency vehicles passed by, she couldn't go on. She turned into an alley and sat down against a wall. Then she erupted into tears. How many times had she cried in the last twenty-four hours? This was different, though. Tears gushed from her eyes with an urgency she'd never experienced before. The fit she'd thrown after dinner the other night suddenly seemed but a childish tantrum. Even the tears she'd shed over Wren and Teal didn't compare. What she was doing now wasn't just crying, Daphna realized. She was *weeping*. She was weeping from a place she never knew existed inside, a place that recognized death—her own death. It was an adult place.

Daphna, her face streaked with dirt and smoke stains and tears, began to sigh with deep, soul-shaking relief. She knew she had to see to her dad. She needed to hug him.

That's who she needed to hug.

She reached into her pocket, hoping to find a tissue, but what she found instead was the note from her mother. It had completely slipped her mind, and she hadn't even read it all! She opened it up and skipped to the part she hadn't read.

The story of this book and the story of my life is long. How I hope to be the one to share it with you! I can't imagine how you might learn the truth without me, but something inside tells me that you will.

You are thirteen today. I will ask your father to give you this note on this day should anything happen to me before it. Use this year to investigate. Search out the story of The First Tongue. Learn about The War of Words.

Savor the triumph of The Eight. Do these things, and you will be prepared for whatever choices lay in your paths.

One more thing, children: if you learn the truth of my life, I beg you not to share it with your father. It would make it more difficult to let me go. The last thing I want is for Milton to waste his life chasing ghosts or grasping for what might be lost. Life is short, after all, no matter how long you live.

Love forever,
Your mother

Daphna carefully folded up the note and put it back into her pocket. There were no more tears now. A single, pitiless feeling was attacking her like a swarm of stinging bees: shame. She felt crippling shame for all the times she'd looked at her mother's less-than-

smooth face in Milton's frames and felt disappointment, for all the times at school she
pretended it was too difficult to write about
her mother because she was dead. Daphna
suddenly saw herself for what she'd been: a
shallow, ignorant, self-absorbed little girl.

"*Daphna?!*"

Someone was yelling her name.

"*Daphna?! Where are you?*"

It was Latty. She was somewhere very
near by. Daphna shrunk down, hoping
against hope she'd not be found.

"You're father's gone by ambulance to
the hospital! He's going to be okay! Where
are you? He told me you were here! Are you
okay? Daphna?! Dexter?!" Latty continued to
call for the twins, but her voice began to fade
a minute later.

Daphna was relieved to get this news
about her father. The poor man! To think
he knew nothing about what was going on!
Nothing about his own wife! Nothing about
the First Tongue or The War of Words or The

triumph of the—*Wait a minute!*

Daphna fumbled the note back out of her pocket and frantically opened it again. She skimmed it over, looking for a line. There it was: *Search out the story of The First Tongue. Learn about the War of Words. Savor the triumph of The Eight.*

"That's not right," Daphna said out loud, leaping to her feet. For once, she remembered an exact detail. Her father would have to wait for that hug.

She took off down the sidewalk, running so single-mindedly that she didn't even hear Latty start screaming her name.

Five minutes later, Daphna burst into the lobby of the R & R, panting. Evelyn Idun was not at her desk, which was fortunate because Daphna wasn't going to stop for anything in the world. She looked an absolute mess and had no idea what she was going to say to explain if she had to. More good luck: the elevator doors were open. Daphna flung herself inside, punched at the buttons and willed the doors to close. The three-floor ride felt excruciatingly long. "*Dex!*" she shouted at the indifferent metal doors. Finally, they slid open. Daphna squeezed out as soon as it was possible and sprinted down the hall.

The door to room 306 was locked.

"Dexter!" Daphna cried, wrenching the knob. She pounded on the door. "Dexter! Don't give her the book!" She put her ear to the door, but couldn't hear anything, but maybe that was because blood was hammering in her head. "Don't give it to her!" she wailed. "It was *The Eight*! *The Eight* defeated Rash and his followers! Don't give her the book, Dex!"

"Daphna?"

Someone was calling to her from the end of the hall. She turned, frantic. It was Mrs. Deucalion. She and Mr. Bergelmir were standing in the hall outside the lounge holding playing cards.

"Have you come back?" Mrs. Deucalion

asked. She was squinting at Daphna, perhaps unsure from a distance what to make of her disheveled state.

Daphna simply ignored the question. She turned back to the door and resumed pounding. "Dex! Dex!"

"Daphna, darling! What's wrong?" This was Mrs. Kunyan, who'd come out of the lounge, too.

"Dex! Don't do it, Dex! It was only eight! She was with *him!*"

A small contingent of Dwarves was now moving slowly down the hall. Daphna looked at them desperately, then turned back again to the infuriating door. *Oh, why did she ever get involved with these annoying little people?!*

"Daphna! You're ill!"

Someone in the group was just a step or two away when the door to room 306 opened abruptly. Daphna was grabbed by the arm and yanked inside.

The door slammed shut behind her.

It was Ruby. With alarming strength for such an old woman, she twisted Daphna's arm and forced her onto the couch. Dex was sitting there, white in the face, his hands trembling in his lap. It was immediately apparent why: Ruby had a gun, a big, old-fashioned revolver, the kind Daphna had seen in gangster movies. She had the book, too.

"Barging in on us again, you little nuisance!" Ruby snapped. Her pleasant, welcoming voice was gone, as was the friendly, motherly look on her cracked and wrinkled face. "Once again your brother and I were having a perfectly fine conversation. I knew all along he'd bring it to me if he got hold of the book. Handed it right over, he did, the little dear."

"She's been telling me not to trust anyone but her," Dex moaned, "not even my family. She must have told me that a hundred times."

Ruby smiled. "Didn't your mother teach you not to listen to strangers? Oh, no—I suppose she never got the chance."

"Rash is dead," Daphna announced,

hoping to knock Ruby off balance.

"I know, and so much the better!" Ruby replied, knocking Daphna off balance instead. "That old fool never understood that open conflict is not the most effective way to get what you want."

Dex and Daphna looked at each other and realized how thoroughly they'd been taken in.

"Asterius was unmanageable from the first," Ruby said. "You aren't as sharp as you'd like to think, little girl. First he almost ruined everything by letting your mother read his mind. Then he throws the precious book off a cliff! Men are such idiots—present company included," she added, winking at Dex.

The twins did not reply, but Ruby evidently wasn't looking for conversation.

"I told you the truth about spying on Asterius," she said. "I've been following him for centuries. He may be a hothead and a fool, but he is relentless after all, and I figured my best bet was to let him find the book and then either rejoin him or simply take it from him. So when he moved here, I moved here, too. And then I saw whom he had that disgusting boy spying on, you two dears. It was obvious to me right away whose children you were, so I decided a recruit was in order. I chose Dex because there is no one easier to manipulate than a boy, angry at the injustices of the cruel, cruel world." She laughed.

Dexter flushed with rage.

"Another of Asterius' problems," Ruby added, "was that he never understood the need to play as many angles as possible. Here's a tip for you, Dexy, from your old tutor: keep your friends close, but keep your enemies closer! One way or another—if your father had it, if Asterius got it, or if you got it from either of them—I've always known I'd get the book back! But don't worry, when I learn the First Tongue, there will be peace. Asterius and I always intended that. After all, what could be more peaceful than a world full of grateful slaves? *Heaven on Earth*, indeed!"

Both Dex and Daphna opened their mouths, but there simply wasn't anything to say. Ruby wasn't done talking anyway.

"And our little part in the story together could have ended so sweetly," she went on. "We could have had a little ceremony in which I burned a book looking a lot like this one, congratulated you two for doing the world a great service, then disappeared into the night for a nice relaxing holiday to read! But no! You've ruined that possibility. I simply can't have you out there looking for me, scheming the way your mother always did.

"No, you've driven me into open conflict, and when Ruby Scharlach is forced into open conflict, things are settled quickly and without a fuss. Let's go. We need to go somewhere private, and Dex, you seem to have a perfect spot. We're going to your little secret hideout in the woods."

murder mystery

Ruby picked up the phone and touched a number. "Evelyn!" she said, sounding like a kindly old lady again. "Is there by any chance a shuttle down there? There is? Fabulous. I've got the Wax twins with me today—Oh, yes, Dexter is here, too. Sure I'll say hi—he'll understand you have to run. We'd like to take a little field trip to Gabriel Park—Yes, the weather. True. We're hoping it rains, actually. Dexter's showing off some sort of Boy Scout talent or other—Great, can he drop us off? Oh, just an hour. Perfect. We'll be right down." Ruby put both the book and gun into her purse, then waved the twins to the door.

"Children," she said, "one false move, as they say, and you're both dead. I'm a crack shot."

Daphna and Dex were both numb now. There seemed to be a limit to the number of times a person could deal with the possibility of being murdered in one day. They simply got up and did as they were told.

But in the hall, Daphna's hopes flickered to life. Mrs. Deucalion and Mr. Bergelmir, along with Mr. Hina and Mrs. Tapi, were there, practically right outside the door. The others were further down the hall, milling around with the goofy looks they always wore. Daphna was sorry she'd wished them away. She was never so glad to see their simple faces! Ruby looked furious at all the traffic.

"Daphna!" Mrs. Tapi said, "I heard you came back. Why, look at you two! You look awful! Is something wrong? Was there a fight? You were shouting."

"Ah—um—actually, we—" Daphna wasn't sure what to say or do. Her instinct was to throw herself at the Dwarves and beg for help, but the poisonous look on Ruby's face silenced her, at least for the moment.

"They do look afright," Ruby said, jovially, as if the twins' bruised and bloodied condition was just their youthful enthusiasm showing.

"You know how kids take their games so seriously," she added. "We're doing one of those murder mystery games, where the players act out parts. Can you believe the make-up? They've just dug up a corpse in the park and have to take me to identify it." Ruby shrugged good-naturedly, as if to say what could she do but indulge such kooky kids.

While the Dwarves took all this in, Daphna looked at each of them with beseeching eyes. Evidently, Ruby saw this because she took the gun out and pointed it at her. "I was going to tell them my part is Double-Crossing Murderer when we got to the park, but this is just too much fun to wait."

The Dwarves had all looked shocked, but then Mr. Bergelmir broke into a grin. "I'd love to play!" he said, his face lighting up. "It's Mrs. Scharlach, yes? I've heard about these games! They even have murder cruise ships these days!"

"I'd love it, too!" This was Mrs. Tapi. Then, all the Dwarves were volunteering to play.

Dex and Daphna looked at each other and shared the same thought. If they could stay in such a large group, they'd be safe. Ruby looked like she could shoot everyone right then and there.

"No," she said, "I wouldn't feel right dragging you all into the woods."

"Oh, but we'd love it!" protested Mrs. Kunyan. "Nothing half this exciting has happened around here in ages! Besides, now that we know you're a Double-Crossing Murderer, we have to protect these poor, innocent children!"

"Of course," Ruby conceded through gritted teeth.

It was agreed, so the Dwarves all shuffled back to their various rooms for coats and hats. In the meantime, Ruby punched at the elevator button, clearly hoping to leave without them. But it wouldn't come. By the time the doors opened, Mr. Dwyfan, whose room was right across the hall, had emerged. He held the elevator while the rest of the group made their plodding way to join him.

Once everyone was finally in, Mr. Hina turned to Daphna. "We can't wait for our next book," he said. "Did you have anything in mind? We're all anxious to know!"

"A murder mystery I hope!" Mr. Bergelmir laughed.

Daphna tried to smile, but it was almost impossible to speak in her current state of mind.

"Oh, I'm still thinking it over," she managed. She pointed at her brother. "This is Dexter," she said, "my twin." This set off a fuss as everyone wanted to get a better look at him.

On the ride over to the park, the Dwarves made eager small talk. They chattered about this and that, mostly to Dex, asking him all about his life. He barely managed replies that kept everyone talking. The Dwarves tried to engage Ruby as well, but she was having none of it.

The bus stopped in a small parking lot abutting the park. When Ruby rose in the aisle, the twins panicked.

Daphna leapt to her feet first and screamed, "This isn't a game! She really is a murderer! It's a real gun!"

'What? What's going on here!" This was the bus driver, turning around in naked alarm.

"You've got to help us!" Dex cried. "She's—" but Ruby was now pointing the gun directly at his heart.

The driver screamed, but the Dwarves all chuckled. One of them went, "Oooooh!" in mock horror.

"Don't worry!" said Mrs. Deucalion. "We're playing Murder Mystery! Look at that make-up—first rate!"

"Get off the bus or die here and now," Ruby said to the twins. They did as they were told, and the group of increasingly amused Dwarves followed. The driver, shaking his head, pulled the door shut behind them and drove away, leaving the whole crowd standing under threatening skies at the head of the park's main trail.

Dex looked down the path at the cedar tree and the spot where he'd blundered into Emmet. That seemed like a thousand years ago.

"Okay, Dex," Ruby said. "Show me where the body is. Any more nonsense, and you'll be joining it in a shallow grave."

"Oh, she's good," Mrs. Kunyan marveled. "She's *really* good."

"We're up to it," said a smiling Mr. Bergelmir. "Here, how about this: Over our dead bodies!"

"That can be arranged," Ruby replied, aiming the gun at him. She flashed a smile.

"She's got us," Mr. Bergelmir admitted.

"Now move, Dexter, or I'll kill you."

Bitterly, Dex led the group down the path. It was slow going with the gang of old people dawdling along, stopping here and there to look for bodies or assassins lurking about. When they passed the giant cedar, Dex veered onto the hidden path diverging into the thick of the woods. The group walked for a good fifteen minutes, pushing aside bushes and branches and stepping over logs. No less than six times, Ruby suggested the gang turn back if the going was too rough, but each time they declined.

After a few more twists among the trees, the Clearing came into view. There was the soft bed of multi-colored leaves. There was the fuzzy moss blanketing the ground. There was the *peace*, thought Dex.

Once in the Clearing, everyone stopped to recuperate and have a look around.

"Ash trees!" Mrs. Kunyan announced. "How absolutely beautiful!" The others concurred, moving around for closer looks.

Ruby could contain herself no longer.

"You forced my hand!" she roared. *"Don't you meddling bunch of old windbags ever SHUT UP?!"*

All talking ceased. Everyone looked stunned.

"Whatever do you mean?" Mr. Dwyfan asked. "Is this part of the game?"

"She means, this isn't a game," Daphna moaned. "We've been trying to tell you. It's a real gun."

Gradually, the Dwarves seemed to comprehend the situation. They looked from Daphna to Ruby, who was regarding them with withering scorn.

"Dexter and Daphna," Ruby instructed, "if either of you make any effort to run, I'll shoot you in the legs and let you die slowly. If you do as I say, I will make it painless."

Neither Dexter nor Daphna replied to this. Neither could.

Ruby turned her attention to the Dwarves. "All of you blowhards, just walk away," she said. "Just go back to your lounge and deal out a new deck of cards."

At first, none of the dwarves moved; they seemed petrified. Then someone moved, Mrs. Tapi, and the whole group followed suit.

They moved, but not away.

Instead, in a bunch, they stepped directly between the twins and Ruby.

"Move!" Ruby repeated. "This is not a game, I promise you!"

But no one did. In fact, they seemed to be hunkering down. It was as if, in the blink of an eye, they'd transformed into some sort of military outfit...

Daphna laughed. She couldn't help herself. She laughed right out loud, and hard. She thought her capacity to show amazement had been exhausted, yet she was amazed. Dex looked at her.

"*The Seven Dwarves*," she whispered, shaking her head, marveling at her apparently infinite dimwittedness. "The triumph of

The Eight. There were *seven* left when Mom died!"

Dex looked at the hunched backs now forming a half circle in front of him. Seven timeworn faces turned and nodded at him solemnly.

Ruby also understood. Her face fell momentarily, but she did not lower the gun.

"I should have known," she sighed. "But no matter! The book is mine, and seven doddering fools can't do a thing about it." She produced the book from her purse and held it aloft.

"It's over, Rose," said Mr. Hina. "Let us have the book."

Ruby, or Rose, laughed outright at this. "Do you think that portentous tone has an effect on me, you ridiculous old man?" she mocked. "I have an offer for you, though. When the Words of Power again pass these lips, I will make you my Overlords. All you have to do is step aside."

There was a long pause, during which

Mr. Hina seemed to be considering the offer. Then he said, oddly, "That's an old-fashioned gun, Rose." He took a step, not to the side, but forward, directly toward Ruby. And then he began walking toward her, like he might approach a friend to shake hands.

With equal parts terror and resignation, Dex and Daphna watched the scene unfold.

When Mr. Hina was just a stride away from Ruby, a gunshot rent the air. At the same moment, a terrific thunderclap burst from the black clouds overhead. Sheets of rain came crashing down over the woods, pelting the Clearing and everyone in it.

Mr. Hina fell to the ground. Dex and Daphna weren't exactly sure what had happened—and now they couldn't see because the six others had stepped together, closing ranks. No one seemed to be speaking, but it was hard to hear anything through the hurtling downpour.

The twins huddled together, uselessly trying to shield each other from the rain.

Soaked already, they cowered behind their aged human shields.

The Dwarves stood steady.

"Give us the book!" one of them shouted. Lightening cracked. A moment later, another spectacular thunderclap.

"You are all fools!" Ruby railed through the rain. "You will all die out here!"

In response to this, the entire group took a deliberate step forward, then another. A second shot rang out. One, two, three, four shots. Or was that thunder? It was booming before, between, after—there was no way to tell what was happening.

The twins dropped to the ground amidst further explosions. More gunshots? More thunder? The sounds were deafening. Brother and sister lay face down in the leaves.

Suddenly, everything went quiet, or seemed to. The sound of steady rain continued, but the thunder, the gunshots, the gutwrenching explosions were gone.

Dex and Daphna sat up, nearly blind with fear. Two figures were left standing in the distance. It was difficult to see clearly through the rain. A mist—or was it smoke?—seemed to have descended. They heard clicking, repeated clicking.

"An old-fashioned six-shooter!" a voice called out. Mrs. Tapi's. "It was over from the start!" she shouted.

"No!" Ruby yelled and took off running. She fell almost immediately over a body. Bodies were everywhere.

The rain suddenly stopped, but sounds were foreign. The landscape was bending. Dex and Daphna saw the lone figure still standing approach the one now getting to its knees. Light flashed from something it took from its pocket.

"Swallow," Mrs. Tapi ordered, but then she added, almost tenderly, "Go in peace."

There was the sound of a brief struggle, then the figure on its knees simply slipped to the ground and lay still.

Things seemed to go in slow motion then. Mrs. Tapi reached down and picked something up from the ground.

The book!

She carried it off to the side of the Clearing, just behind the twins, who did not, at first, turn to face her. There was the sound of a match being struck, then another. A voice then: Mrs. Tapi's again.

"Do not grieve," she whispered. "Do not for a moment lament the melancholy events that have occurred in this place.

"When your mother informed us of her intention to abandon the search to raise a family, we were saddened, but not surprised. Several of us did the very same thing over the years, though our own tragedies brought each of us back. We were saddened to learn of her death, and we agreed to establish a watch over you in gratitude for all she had done. At least one of us has been here ever since, but we all came together recently to spend our final days together.

"Daphna, our plan was to reveal ourselves to you on your visit to us today, on
your birthday, and ask you to bring Dexter to
us, too. We hoped to recruit you to the search.
We had no idea what was going on under our
noses, I am ashamed to admit. Please do not
be angry with us. Ruby looks nothing like
she used to. Mr. Bergelmir saw you enter her
room. It was we who triggered the building's
alarm in hopes of discovering what was going on. We had little strength left, but enough
for a moment like this. The only thing we all
craved as much as completing our mission
was an end to our wearied lives. Now, at long
last, we have accomplished both. I will destroy this book once and for all. If I could just
get a fire start—"

Mrs. Tapi's voice hitched. She was suddenly gasping for air. Dex and Daphna finally
turned. Time sped up. The forest spun; everything blurred.

Something inhuman. A monstrosity. A
bulging and bloated beast with wet, red skin,

if the thing could be said to have skin at all, had Mrs. Tapi by the throat.

Neither Dex nor Daphna were sure they were seeing what they thought they were seeing—how could they be? Both were sure what they smelled though. A putrid odor was radiating from the thing. Daphna tried to turn away, but found it impossible. Dex began to gag. It was dark; it was raining again; they had to be hallucinating. Mrs. Tapi wasn't even struggling. She was limp. The thing let go of her, and she slumped to the forest floor.

Now it was coming toward them.

It was all too unreal. Neither twin moved. The thing was standing over them. Now it was keeling between them. Wet hands were pressing down on their throats. Then a voice, ruined, croaked, "It was the old man. Then it was that old lady, and now it's gonna be—"

That's when the screaming started. Words weren't discernible, only raw, primal screaming. Someone was running and screaming toward the Clearing. The thing let go of their throats. It scrambled along the ground. Then it ran.

Now there were sirens again, and the sounds of lots of people shouting among the trees. Colors blended and dripped.

Everything faded to black.

words

Dexter tried to open his eyes. With significant effort, he managed to open the left, but the right was swollen shut. His lip was puffed up and crusty and throbbing, and his limbs felt like dead weights. He was dry, though, lying in a bed wearing ugly green pajamas. Daphna was blinking at him from another bed, wearing the same thing.

"We're in the hospital," she whispered. "You've been asleep for hours! The police were here. I was pretending to be asleep so I wouldn't have to say anything. *They're all dead*, Dex. *All of them*. I've been looking down on them, on old people, for—forever, acting like I was some great person for taking pity on them. I feel like I woke up from the worst nightmare of all time." Daphna blinked again, then began to sob.

"They were so good to me, so kind and caring," she whimpered. "They're dead, Dex. *Dead*. Even if they were ready to go, *they're dead*."

"That thing," Dex said. "It was—"

"Emmet. He finally got his wish."

"But that fire—how could he have survived?"

"I don't know."

"Is Dad here?"

"Yeah," Daphna said. "He got hurt, Dex—really bad. Emmet did it! Dad fractured his hip and had to have surgery. And he got a concussion, too. I think he's been acting weird, mumbling strange stuff or something. I'm not sure 'cause they went in the hall to talk about him. He's in a room somewhere with Latty now I guess. And Dex, *it was Latty who found us*. She put Dad in an ambulance and went looking for us. She chased me all over the neighborhood!

"She found Evelyn at the R & R and they

drove to the park. Dex, she saved our lives. Emmet was going to kill us for sure. Dex," Daphna added, "I was so scared, I peed in my pants."

Dexter nodded, but did not comment. "What about all that money?" he whispered.

Daphna shrugged. "I'm sure there's a—" she started to say, but just then, Latty came in.

At the sight of the twins awake, she broke into tears and rushed at them. But she stopped short of taking them into her arms. She backed up, weeping with relief. "Dex, Daphna!" she cried, "I'm—I'm so sorry."

"It's okay," Dex said, but with no irritation. "We're okay."

"And you were right," Daphna admitted. "You were right to be worried. You were right about Rash. In fact, you have no idea how right you were. I'd understand if you never let us out of the house again."

"No," Latty said, surprising the twins, "I've been wrong, absolutely wrong. Hearing that horrid name again sent me into an awful state thinking about your mother. But, kids, I should never have told you my promise to her. I shouldn't have burdened you with it. It was selfish and weak of me to try to manage you with guilt. I've been a smothering presence in your lives for far too long."

The twins looked at each other.

"But," said Dex, "if you weren't chasing after us, we'd be—"

"If I wasn't so controlling, you might not have felt the need to defy me."

"It's okay, Latty," Daphna said. "You're not *that* controlling. Okay, you are, but we know you love us—like we were your own kids."

That Latty was touched deeply by this was obvious. Her very person seemed to light up.

"From now on things will be different," she promised. "I give you my word on it. Deal?" she asked.

"Deal."

Latty couldn't help herself. She swooped upon the beds and swept both twins into a wrenching hug. The twins gave one back.

When Latty finally let them go, they said, simultaneously, "Can we go see, Dad?"

"Of course!" Latty said. "But let me get the doctor first, and the police want to talk to you, too."

Fortunately, everyone believed the twins had passed out after the first gunshot, and that they had no idea what was going on, that they'd just been in the wrong place at the wrong time when an old woman went off her rocker. And no one had gotten a close look at the figure who'd fled the scene. An investigation was underway.

Without arousing suspicion, Daphna managed to ask if there was any connection between what happened to them and the fire at the bookstore, and even slipped in a question about whether any books had been found in the Clearing. In both cases, the answer was no.

On the walk over to Milton's room, Latty explained that Evelyn Idun was arranging to have him transferred to the Home for rehabilitation. Neither Dex nor Daphna listened closely to the details. They stopped at a door.

"Can we—" Daphna started to say. "I mean, would you mind if we see Dad alone?"

"Of course not!" Latty said. "But wait—"

The twins paused and looked at her expectantly.

"Your father will be asleep," she said, "but he told me something in the car on the way over to that store. He's realized some things himself."

"What?" the twins asked.

"He thinks he's botching his role as a father."

The twins flashed each other a look. There was no animosity, only relief.

"He realized he's investing too much of himself in books and too little in you," Latty explained. "He admitted to me that it's been his way of keeping your mother with him all these years. But after seeing how distant you two have grown during this last trip, he decided it's just not worth the price. He said he didn't even know why he felt compelled to stay away this summer—though he suspects it had something to do with not wanting your birthday to come, not wanting you to become young adults when he'd so long looked forward to celebrating the day with your mother here, too. That's why he didn't get any gifts, kids."

"But, if Dad retires—" Daphna asked, eyeing her brother surreptitiously. "I know we have some money from Mom—but won't he have to work a little?"

Latty didn't respond at first. She just looked concerned. "Oh, honey!" she said. "That's not something we should even think about right now. Everything is over. Let's bury the past first, then we'll worry about the future." No one spoke for a moment, but then Latty smiled tenderly. "I'll be right there for both of you," she said.

Dex braced himself to see his father bolted into some sort of hideous contraption. Daphna was prepared for a giant cast right up to his waist. But when they walked into the room, they both sighed. The only evidence of their father's injury and operation was a wheelchair sitting next to his bed. On the other hand, Milton looked like a shell of his former self.

"Dad?" Dex whispered, somehow fearing a loud voice would shatter his father to bits.

Milton didn't respond.

Daphna looked down sadly at this scarcely recognizable man on the bed. Was this broken figure really her father, the man she'd followed into a thousand mysterious and enchanting bookstores? The thought struck her that he was going to be out of commission for a long time. And this thought was followed by a piercing insight. Since Daphna was a little girl, she had always—somewhere in the back of her mind—worried it could come to this. Her mother vanished, and didn't that mean her father might very well vanish, too? And now, in a very real way, it seemed he had. Daphna understood that she'd spent most her life so far fashioning herself into someone who could fend for herself. Being the expert meant not depending on anyone. On impulse, Daphna rushed to her father, leaned over and hugged him hard, and she kept hugging him even though he made no effort to hug her back.

Dex watched his sister with her arms around their father and realized how much she needed him. And then all at once, he understood why he'd kept insisting his father didn't care about them. If his dad didn't care about him, he wouldn't have to care back. No, that wasn't quite it. He wouldn't have to care about *himself*. It was just the opposite of the way he'd made himself see Ruby. It suddenly struck him that if his life was a book, so far it probably made about as much sense as the Book of Nonsense.

When Daphna straightened up, he said, "How did you figure it out? I mean about Ruby and The Eight?"

"Oh, you haven't seen it!" Daphna fished the now badly crumpled note out of the breast pocket of her hospital pajamas.

"Here, read this," she said, holding it out for Dex. He made no move to take the note. "Oh, right!" Daphna said, flushing. She read the note out loud.

"Dex," Daphna said when she finished, "there's something I still don't understand. When Rash was using your eyes, when he saw the book we messed up—"

"Why did he still think it was his?"

"Yeah."

"I was trying to tell you, in Dad's room, before Emmet barged in. When I look at words, they move. It's like they all flip around and drop off the end of lines. I was pretty sure, if it came to it, Rash would believe it. Since I remembered that nonsense line you read, I felt pretty safe about the whole thing."

This struck brother and sister as funny. They both laughed.

Then Daphna said, "Dexter, I'm—I'm sorry."

Dex looked at her blankly, as if waiting for something. Finally, he said, "But—?"

"What do you mean?" Daphna asked.

"Whenever you say you're sorry, you say 'but,'" Dex explained, "as in 'but it's really all your fault.'"

Daphna flushed again. "I'm sorry for that, too," she said. It suddenly struck her that if life was a book, she'd understood it about as well as the Book of Nonsense. "But I'm really, really sorry for the way I've looked down on you," she added. "And I also want to say thanks."

"For—for what?" Dex asked.

"For what you did in Dad's room, for thinking so fast, for facing Emmet that way. I know he hurt you, Dex. You're a million times braver than I am. I actually threw up. All I do anymore is cry and puke and wet myself."

Dexter, completely embarrassed but completely grateful, didn't know how to reply.

Daphna, to her surprise, reached for her brother's hand. To her even greater surprise, he let her take it. And it was at that moment she realized something else: you didn't need to speak the First Tongue to utter magic words.

"Dex," she said.

"Yeah?"

"Emmet got the book. It's still out there."

"Which means the Councilors died for nothing."

"We need to get it back, Dex. We need to destroy it. Will you help?"

Dex looked at his sister. "I give you my word," he said.

"What is it?" Daphna asked. "I mean, your 'word,' what is it? I've never understood that expression."

"Me neither," Dex admitted, "but my word is 'Quack.'"

Daphna grinned. "I'll take it," she replied.

"And I give you my word. It's 'Galice!'"

"I'll take it," Dex replied.

The twins nodded at one another. Still holding hands, they turned to look at their father again.

"What if he doesn't get better?" Dex worried.

"He will," Daphna promised.

"I hope you're—" Dex started to say, but he stopped because Milton was stirring. Gingerly, he rolled over. Then he slowly opened his eyes.

When Milton Wax saw his children, he smiled. The twins smiled back.

No words were necessary.